'Jane,' Cade whispered. 'You gonna let her stop us, let her keep us from each other?'

She was looking at his mouth. So dangerous. So exactly what she longed for. She realised she was biting the inside of her lower lip. She made herself stop. 'It's not only my mother.'

'What else?'

'You know what,' Jane answered. 'We don't want the same things.'

'That's right.' The very sound of Cade's voice was like a tender hand, stroking. 'We do want different things. I want *you*. You want *me*.'

'Very funny.' She wasn't laughing. 'I mean we want different things in life. So this can't go anywhere.'

'Is it so necessary for a love affair to *go* somewhere?' Cade asked.

'Not as long as you're having that love affair with someone who isn't me.'

'But, Jane,' he answered, 'I thought you understood. I don't want to have a love affair with someone who isn't you.'

Available in October 2003 from Silhouette Special Edition

Mercury Rising
by Christine Rimmer
(The Sons of Caitlin Bravo)

His Marriage Bonus
by Cathy Gillen Thacker
(The Deveraux Legacy)

The Cupcake Queen
by Patricia Coughlin

Willow in Bloom
by Victoria Pade
(The Coltons)

My Very Own Millionaire
by Pat Warren
(2-in-1)

The Woman for Dusty Conrad
by Tori Carrington

Mercury Rising

CHRISTINE RIMMER

SILHOUETTE®
SPECIAL EDITION™

*First published in Great Britain 2003
Silhouette Books, Eton House, 18-24 Paradise Road,
Richmond, Surrey TW9 1SR*

© Christine Rimmer 2002

ISBN 0 373 24496 7

23-1003

*Printed and bound in Spain
by Litografia Rosés S.A., Barcelona*

For my nieces
Lily and Tessa and Morgan,
with all my love.

CHRISTINE RIMMER

came to her profession the long way around. Before
settling down to write about the magic of romance,
she'd been an actress, a sales assistant, a janitor,
a model, a phone sales representative, a teacher, a
waitress, a playwright and an office manager. She
insists she never had a problem keeping a job—she was
merely gaining 'life experience' for her future as a
novelist. Christine is grateful not only for the joy she
finds in writing, but for what waits when the day's work
is through: a man she loves, who loves her right back,
and the privilege of watching their children grow and
change day to day. She lives with her family in
Oklahoma.

SILHOUETTE®
SPECIAL EDITION™

*is proud to present the all-new trilogy continuing
the Bravo family saga from*

CHRISTINE RIMMER

THE SONS OF CAITLIN BRAVO

Aaron, Cade and Will—
can any woman tame them?

HIS EXECUTIVE SWEETHEART
August 2003

MERCURY RISING
October 2003

SCROOGE AND THE SINGLE GIRL
December 2003

Chapter One

"**M**om?"

Virginia Elliott turned from the window. "Ah. Thank you, dear." Jane gave her the fresh-cut blush-pink roses she'd just wrapped in a cone of newspaper. "So lovely…" Virginia brought them close, breathed in their scent. "You do have a way in the garden. Your aunt Sophie would be proud."

Jane's beloved Aunt Sophie Elliott had been a single lady all her life. When she'd died, nearly three years ago now, she left Jane her beautiful old house and the gorgeous garden surrounding it.

Her mother turned back to the window. "I notice your new neighbor is at home."

"Yes." Jane kept her voice and her expression as bland as a clean white sheet. "He does travel a lot, though."

Virginia had the roses in her left hand. Her right strayed to the pearls at her throat. She fondled them, ticking them off like the beads of a rosary. "He was out there, on the side porch, just a moment ago." Each word was heavy with disdain.

Jane resisted the urge to say something sarcastic. *Well, Mother. It* is *his house. I suppose he has the right to be out on the porch.*

Word around town was that Cade Bravo owned an ostentatious new house in Las Vegas and a condo in nearby Lake Tahoe. He'd taken the small town of New Venice completely by surprise when he'd bought the Lipcott place next-door to Jane's. A run-down farmhouse-style Victorian seemed the last place he would ever want to live.

But the house wasn't run-down anymore. Renovations had gone on for months. Finally the various work crews had picked up and moved on and the new owner had taken up residence.

"At least he had the grace to respect the integrity of the original home," Virginia said grudgingly, hand still at her pearls.

Jane thought he had done a beautiful job with the old house. It looked much as it must have when it was first built, at the turn of the last century, a house a lot like Jane's house, one that harkened back to simpler, more graceful times, with an inviting deep wraparound porch and fish scale shingles up under the eaves.

Virginia muttered, "Still. One of those Bravo boys living on Green Street. Who ever could have imagined such a thing?" Green Street was wide and tree-lined. The charming old houses on it had always been owned by respectable and prosperous members of the New Venice community, people from well-established local families—the Elliotts and the Chases, the Moores and the Lipcotts.

True, Cade Bravo had surprised everyone by prospering. In that sense, he fit the profile for a resident of Green Street. Was he respectable? Not by Virginia Chase Elliott's exacting standards. But then, in Virginia's thoroughly biased opinion, no Bravo was—or ever could be—considered respectable.

"Does he bother you, honey?" Her mother was looking right at her now.

"Of course not."

"He was always such a wild one—the worst of the bunch, everyone says so. Takes after that mother of his." Virginia's gray eyes narrowed when she mentioned Caitlin Bravo. Her hand worried all the harder at her pearls. "I suppose he's got the women in and out all the time."

"No. He's very quiet, actually, when he's here—and you should get those roses home. Cut an inch off the stems, at a slant, and—"

Her mother waved the hand that had been so busy with the pearls. "I know, I know. Remove any leaves below the waterline."

Jane smiled. "That's right. And use that flower food I gave you."

Virginia sighed. "I will, I will—and how is Celia?"

Celia Tuttle was one of Jane's two closest friends. Her name was Celia Bravo now. A little over two months ago, at the end of May, Celia had married Cade's oldest brother, Aaron.

"Happy," said Jane. "Celia is very, very happy."

One of Virginia's eyebrows inched upward. "Pregnant, or so I heard."

"Yes. She and Aaron are thrilled about that."

"I meant, a little *too* pregnant for how long they've been married."

Jane shook her head. "Mother. Give it up. Celia is *happy.* Aaron loves her madly. They are absolutely adorable together, totally devoted—and looking forward to having a baby. *I'd* like to find a man who loves me the way Aaron Bravo loves his wife."

Her mother made a prim noise in her throat. Jane folded her arms and gave Virginia a long, steady look heavily freighted with rebuke.

Virginia relented. She waved her hand again. "All right, all right. Celia is a sweet girl and if she's happy, I'm happy *for* her."

"So good of you to say so."

"Don't get that superior tone, please. I don't like it when you do that—and I know, I know. Celia is your dearest friend in the world, along with Jillian." Jane and Celia and Jillian Diamond had been best friends since kindergarten. "I ought to have sense enough never to say a word against either of them."

"Yes, you should."

Virginia stepped closer, the look in her eyes softening. She reached out and smoothed Jane's always-wild hair in a gesture so tender, so purely maternal that Jane couldn't help but be soothed by it. Jane did love her mother, though Virginia was not always easy to love.

"You haven't mentioned how your date went Friday."

Jane gave her mother a noncommittal smile. "I had a nice time."

Virginia looked pained. "My. Your indifference is nothing short of stunning."

Indifference. Sadly that pretty much summed up Jane's feelings about Friday night. It had been her second date with that particular man. He taught Science at the high school and Jane had met him over a year ago now. He'd come into her bookstore looking for a good manual on Sierra birds and a well-illustrated book on weather patterns. He really did seem the kind of man she'd been looking for: steady and trustworthy, kind and wise. A man who had sought to be her friend first. He'd told her he admired her straightforwardness, said he respected her independence and valued her intelligence. Jane believed him when he said those things.

And he was nice-looking, too, with thick brown hair and a muscular build. There was nothing *not* to like about him. Jane *did* like him. She also knew in her heart that liking was all she felt for him.

Was she asking too much in daring to want it all—decency and steadiness *and* a kiss that turned her inside out?

Probably.

"Gary Nevis is a great guy, Mom. I just don't think he's the guy for me."

"Now. Give it time. You might discover there's more there than you realized."

"Good advice," Jane agreed without much enthusiasm.

"And on that note, I'll take my roses and go home."

Jane walked her mother out the door and down the front steps.

"A beautiful summer we're having," her mother said as they proceeded down the walk toward the car at the curb.

"Oh, yes." Jane turned her face up to the warm ball of the August sun. "A splendid summer." Northern Nevada's Comstock Valley was, in Jane's admittedly biased opinion, the best place in the entire world to live. A place where the pace of life was not too hectic, where you knew your neighbors, where people were always forgetting to lock their doors and it never mattered because nothing bad every happened. Here, folks enjoyed reasonably mild winters and summers where daytime temperatures tended to max out in the low eighties.

At the curb, about twenty feet from the low, celadon-green sports car parked in front of Cade's house, Jane took the roses and held the door open while her mother got settled into her Town Car, sliding onto the soft leather seat and taking the sunscreen out of the windshield, folding it neatly and stowing it in back.

"Here. Give me those." Virginia took the bundle of fragrant pink blooms, turned to lay it carefully on the passenger seat to her right, then smiled up at her daughter once more. "Thank you for coming to church with me."

"I enjoyed it."

"And for the lunch."

"My pleasure."

Virginia lifted her cheek for a kiss.

Jane fondly obliged. Then she stepped back and swung the door shut. Her mother fumbled in the console for a moment, came up with the key and stuck it in the ignition. A moment later, the big car sailed off down the street, turning at the corner onto Smith Way and rolling on out of sight.

Jane turned back toward her house. She got about two steps and paused to admire the scene before her.

Her house was Queen Anne-style. It had a turret with a spire on top, touches of gingerbread trim in the eaves and a multitude of cozy nooks and crannies.

Her garden stole her breath. It was late-summer glorious now, a little overblown, like a beautiful woman just past her prime. The Jack clematis that climbed the side fence was in full flower. Black-eyed Susans thrust their gold-petaled faces up to meet the sun. The big patch of lacy-leaved cosmos to the right of her walk was a riot of purple, white, lavender and pink.

Among the cosmos, on pedestals of varying heights, Jane had mounted a series of gazing balls, one blue, one pink, one green, one that looked like a huge soap bubble, crystal clear with just the faintest sheen of mother-of-pearl. The cosmos partially masked them. They peeked out, smooth reflective spheres, giving back the gleam of sunlight.

Oh, it was all so very lovely. If she didn't have her dear aunt Sophie anymore, at least she had a house and a garden that filled her heart to bursting every time she took a minute to stop and really look at it.

Jane let out a small laugh of pure pleasure. Enough with basking in delight at the beauty that surrounded her. She needed to put on her old clothes and her wide straw hat and get after it. With the bookstore closed, Sunday was prime time for working in the yard. She had the rest of the day completely to herself—and the tomatoes and carrots out back cried out for harvesting.

She started up the walk again—and spotted Cade Bravo, just emerging from the shadows of his porch.

She hadn't meant to look toward his house, she truly hadn't.

But somehow, she'd done it anyway. And as her glance found him, he emerged into the sunlight, those long, strong legs of his moving fast, down the steps, along the walk.

The sunlight caught in his hair. Oh, he did have beautiful hair—not brown and not gold, but some intriguing color in between, hair that made a woman want to get her fingers in it. He kept it short, but it had a seductive tendency to curl. Jane secretly thought it was the kind of hair a Greek god might have, hair suitable for crowning with a laurel wreath.

He waved, just a casual salute of a motion, long fingers to his forehead, so briefly, then dropping away as he moved on by.

"Hi, Cade." She gave him a quick cool smile, ignoring the shiver that slid beneath the surface of her skin, pretending she didn't feel the heat that pooled in her belly, that she didn't notice the sudden acceleration of her pulse rate.

Turning away in relief and despair, Jane made for the haven of her house.

Chapter Two

Cade got past Jane and went on down the walk. He had hardly glanced at her, just given her that quick wave and moved on by.

He knew that was how she wanted it. So fine. Let her have what she wanted.

It wouldn't have been such a bright idea to try to get her talking right then, anyway. He was on edge. Who could say what dangerous things might slip out of his mouth? The sight of Virginia Elliott, staring at him through Jane's dining-room window, fingering her pearls and scowling, had pretty much ruined his day.

Cade got in his car, slammed the door and started the engine. He wanted a drink. But he didn't want to sit by himself in the house he probably never should have bought, pouring shots and knocking them back.

Drinking alone was just too depressing. So he was headed for the Highgrade, a combination saloon/café/gift shop/gaming establishment on Main Street. Headed for home—or at least, the closest thing to home he'd every known. He'd grown up there, in the rambling apartment above the action, on the second floor.

Flat-roofed and sided in clapboard, the Highgrade was paneled inside in never-ending knotty pine. Slots lined the walls and the air smelled of greasy burgers, stale beer and too many cigarettes.

Okay, there had to be better places for a man in need of cheering up to go. But even on Sunday, he knew he'd find a few die-hard regulars in the bar. They wouldn't be big talkers. He'd be lucky to get a few grunts and a "Hiya, Cade." But technically at least, he wouldn't be drinking alone.

It was a very short drive to Main Street. Cade swung into the alley between the Highgrade and Jane's store, Silver Unicorn Books.

Jane. The name echoed like a taunt in his brain.

Seemed he couldn't turn around lately without being reminded of her. Ubiquitous. That was the word for her.

And don't laugh. Yeah, maybe he hadn't been to college—like Jane. And like both of his brothers. But he could read. And set goals. He tried to learn a new word for every weekday. Five new words a week. Times fifty-two. Do the math. Two hundred sixty new words a year. Including ubiquitous, which was another word for Jane.

Because she was *everywhere*. She had the store

next to his mother's place. One of her two closest friends had married his brother. And she lived in the house beside his.

Yeah, yeah. If living next to her bothered him, he shouldn't have bought the damn house in the first place.

But he'd had that itch to move back home. And he'd scratched it by buying the old Lipcott place. How the hell was he supposed to know what was going to happen to him as a result of buying a damn house? How was he going to know ahead of time that proximity would breed awareness? And that awareness would develop into a yen.

It just wasn't the kind of thing that he'd ever imagined could happen to him. Uh-uh. Cade Bravo didn't brood over lovers—or over women he wished would become his lovers.

Why should he? In spite of his lack of formal education, women liked him just fine. He'd never had to put up with a whole lot of rejection. Most women were willing to look at him twice. And besides, he'd always been a guy who took life as it came. If a woman didn't respond to him, well, hey, guess what? There'd be someone new on the horizon real soon.

He'd never been the type to pine and yearn.

Or at least, he hadn't until now.

Cade parked his car in one of the spaces reserved for family at the rear of the building and went in through the back door.

Caitlin Bravo had owned the Highgrade for over thirty years, since before Cade was born. The way Cade understood it, his bad dad, Blake Bravo, had set her up with it. The old man had given her three sons and the Highgrade and then vanished from their lives, never to be seen by any of them again.

In fact, Cade had never seen his father, period—not in the flesh anyway, only in pictures. It was no source of pride to him that he was the only one of Caitlin's three sons who had his daddy's eyes. Silvery eyes. Scary eyes, a lot of folks thought.

And let's lay it on the table here, the old man had been a pretty scary guy.

Blake Bravo had faked his own death in an apartment fire not all that long after he'd planted the seed that would one day be Cade. And later, once everyone thought he was dead, he had kidnapped his own brother's second son, claimed a huge ransom—and never returned the child.

The way everyone figured it now, in hindsight, Blake must have put some poor loser's body in his place when he burned that apartment building down. And somehow, he must have managed to falsify dental records. He'd been out on bail at the time, up on a manslaughter charge after killing some other luckless fool in a barroom brawl.

Getting dead had made it possible for him to beat the manslaughter rap without even going to trial. One clever guy, that Blake Bravo.

The good news was, Blake was really and truly dead now. He'd died in an Oklahoma hospital a little over a year ago. Embarrassed the hell out of Caitlin, to learn that the dead guy she'd always considered the love of her life had lived an extra thirty years and then some beyond what she'd known about.

Inside the Highgrade, things were hopping on the café side. It was usually that way on Sundays after church. Caitlin, in skintight jeans and a spangled Western shirt, was playing hostess, leading people to the booths, ringing them up at the register when they were ready to go. She saw him and gave him a wink.

He went the other way, into the comforting morose silence of the bar.

Bertha was bartending. Big and solid with carrot-colored braids anchored in a crown around her head, Bertha didn't talk much. She had a good heart and a ready smile. Cade had never known a Highgrade without Bertha Slider working there.

"Hey, honeybunch." One look in his face and Bertha knew what to do. She put the bottle of Cuervo on the bar with a shot glass beside it, set out the lime wedges and the salt, poured the beer chaser.

There were two other guys down the bar a ways. Cade saluted them and got the expected pair of grunts in response. He fisted his hand, licked the side of it and poured on the salt. Then he knocked back the first shot.

It was no good, he realized about an hour later. He'd only had a couple of shots, after all, hadn't even gotten himself to the stage where his lips started feeling numb.

And he didn't want any more. Didn't want to get drunk.

Things had gotten pretty bad when a man didn't even have the heart to pour a river of tequila over his sorrows. He tossed a twenty on the bar, said goodbye to Bertha and got the hell out.

He knew he shouldn't have, but he went back to his house. Somehow, while those two shots and that one beer to chase them hadn't made him even close to drunk, they *had* broken through his determination to put the book-peddling temptress next door out of his mind. He stopped in front of his house and turned off the engine and just sat there behind the wheel, staring at her front yard where flowers of every kind and color twined the fences and lined the walk.

He didn't see her. She must be in back. He knew she was out in that yard of hers somewhere. It was her gardening day.

Sundays, as a rule, she went to church with her mother. And after that, she would go out and work in the yard. Sometimes she wore a huge, ugly straw hat. But sometimes she didn't. Sometimes, she'd go bare-headed, anchoring that wildly curling coffee-colored hair in a tumbling knot on her head. Always, for working in the yard, she wore baggy old clothes that somehow, to him, seemed all the more provocative for what they didn't reveal.

Yeah, all right. He knew her habits. He knew her ways.

He'd observed her going in and out of her house morning, afternoon and evening, headed to and from that bookstore of hers, all that hair loose on her shoulders, snaky tendrils of it lifted and teased by the wind.

She often left her windows open. He could hear her in there sometimes, talking on the phone in that soft alto voice of hers. Her laughter was low, musical…warm.

The sound of her had the same effect on him as the sight of her. It made him think of getting her naked and burying his face in all that hair—of listening to that gorgeous voice of hers pitched to a whisper, saying wicked things meant for his ears alone.

He knew damn well she had a wild side. He also knew she kept it under strictest control. Ask anyone. They'd tell you. Since Rusty Jenkins died seven or eight years back in a botched convenience store robbery, Jane Elliott had strictly walked the straight and narrow. She'd gone to Stanford after Rusty died, got herself a nice liberal arts degree. She had her garden and her auntie's house and her cute little bookstore on Main Street. She dated only upwardly mobile guys with steady jobs. She was thoroughly practical, completely down-to-earth and obstinately sensible.

Cade, on the other hand, had made his money in poker parlors up and down the state and later, in the big tournaments in Las Vegas and L.A. And yeah, he'd been in a few tight scrapes with the law—most of them while he was in his teens and early twenties, back when Jane's uncle, J. T. Elliott, who was now the mayor, had been the sheriff. He also had that rep as a lady-killing charmer. And yeah, all right. He'd admit it. The rep was mostly earned.

Jane Elliott, unfortunately, was the one sort of woman a guy like Cade didn't really have a prayer with—and he knew it. She was the kind who'd been there and done that and learned from her mistakes. If he had any sense at all, he'd forget her.

But hey. Who said sense had a damn thing to do with it?

He was suffering, and it was bad. And since his brother had married Jane's friend Celia, it had only gotten worse. Now, he and Jane sometimes ended up at the same social events.

And don't think he hadn't tried to make use of the opportunity those events provided. He'd been no slouch. He'd tried all the preliminary moves a man will use on a woman who attracts him. He'd stood a little too close—and she had backed away. He'd struck up achingly casual conversations—which she concluded quickly and politely before they even really got started. When there was food available, he'd offered to bring her a plateful. What he got for that was a cool smile and a "Thanks, Cade. I'm not hungry right now."

Once, there was dancing. He asked her to dance. She surprised the hell out of him by following him out onto the floor. He held her in his arms—for one dance, and one dance only. Her spectacular breasts rubbed against his chest. The scent of her hair almost drove him insane.

The minute the music stopped she thanked him and pulled free.

Before she could escape, he'd suggested, "Hey. How about one more?"

For that, he got a wry twisting of her wide mouth and a maddeningly arousing low chuckle. "I'm not really a big one for dancing, Cade."

He knew she wasn't interested—or if maybe she

was interested, she would never give her interest a chance to become anything more.

He'd had enough women come on to him over the years to realize when one was *not* coming on, when she wasn't even willing to sit back and relax and let *him* come on to her.

It was probably nothing short of hopeless, the yearning inside him that tied him in knots.

So why the hell did it keep getting stronger?

He knew where this had to lead. That the moment was fast approaching when he would come right out and ask her. Give it to her point-blank: *Jane. Will you go out with me?*

He'd just been putting it off for as long as he could stand it. After all, he knew what would happen when he asked her. She would turn him down flat.

The day was really heating up. Cade shrugged out of his leather jacket, tossed it on the passenger seat.

Then he got out of the car. This craziness had to end.

He would ask the question now, today. She'd give him her answer.

And then, just maybe, he could get over Jane Elliott and get on with his life.

Chapter Three

Jane had picked the ripest tomatoes. They waited in a basket on the porch steps. She'd pulled up a bucketful of carrots, shaking the fragrant black soil off of them and sticking them just inside the back door, ready to clean up later, when she was done outside for the day.

For about thirty-five minutes, she'd been squatting among the rows, digging up persistent dandelions and other irritating weeds. Her back was feeling the strain.

With a small groan, she stood, pulling off her grimy gardening gloves, dropping them at her feet. Sweat had collected under her straw hat, so she skimmed it off and raked her hand back through her unruly hair, letting the slight afternoon breeze cool her off a little. She grabbed the boat neckline of her old shirt and fanned it. It felt wonderful, that cool air flowing down her shirt. Then she put her hand at the base of her spine and rubbed a little.

Oh, yes. Much better....

"Jane."

She froze. She didn't have to turn and look to know who it was. She knew his voice, would have known it anywhere. Deep and soft and rough, all at the same time, the voice she sometimes heard calling her in her dreams.

In her dreams, she always called back, *Yes, oh yes!* And sometimes, in her dreams, he found her and took her in his arms. Just before he kissed her, the dream would fade. And then, usually, she would wake. She would stare at the ceiling and fight the urge to go to the window, to see if the lights were on at his house.

She hadn't heard him come through the back gate. How long had he watched her?

Her legs felt kind of shaky. And a flush crept up her cheeks. But she couldn't stand there, looking off toward the back fence forever.

He had to be faced.

She turned. He was waiting maybe fifteen feet away, not far from her back porch. In those wonderful, deliciously frightening silver eyes of his, she could see what he planned to say to her.

She supposed she had known it was coming. She opened her mouth, to get it over with, to tell him no before he even got a chance to ask the question. But she shut it without speaking.

Something had happened in his face. Something tender and vulnerable, something that yearned as she yearned.

All right, whatever he felt for her deep in his secret heart, he was going to have to get over it. Just as she fully intended to get over him. Cade Bravo was not Rusty Jenkins—thank God. But he was close enough. A wild-hearted Bravo man, a lady-killer who lived the gambler's life, dangerous to love for any woman.

But especially for a woman like Jane who'd let love—or desire, or lust or whatever you wanted to call it—almost annihilate her once and had sworn never to let anything like that happen again, a woman who had a nice, stable life now and was not in the market for anything even remotely resembling a tumultuous affair.

What Jane sought in a man, Cade Bravo didn't have.

And yet, to be fair to him, she had to admit he'd handled himself with courtesy and tact. For months, he had kept his distance. Yes, she'd known he watched her. But how could she blame him for that, when she was doing the same thing herself? Watching him right back, wishing it might be different…

He'd done all the right things whenever they ended up at the same party or get-together. He'd let her know he was interested. But he hadn't pushed her. The minute she'd made her reluctance clear, he had backed off.

And now, when he was finally making a real move, he had a right to a little courtesy from her. He deserved to be treated with respect.

Nervously she fingered the brim of her straw hat, aware of the moisture between her breasts and beneath her arms, of the way her hair clung to the back of her neck, of the bead of sweat that was sliding down her temple, almost to her cheekbone now. "Listen." She lifted one hand, carefully, and wiped away that bead of sweat. "Would you like to go inside? I've got some iced tea in the fridge. I could maybe even dig up a beer, if you'd prefer that."

Those silver eyes regarded her. They saw down into the depths of her. They saw things she wished they didn't.

"Inside?" he asked softly. The one word meant a hundred things, most of them sexual, all of them dangerous.

Too late to back out now. She bent, picked up her dirty gloves. "Yes. What do you say?"

He took a moment to answer. She found herself watching his mouth—the mouth she never quite got to kiss in her dreams. The mouth, she reminded herself sternly, that she had better start forgetting about. And soon.

"Yeah," he said at last. "Iced tea sounds great."

Another silence, between them. A silence that felt like a standoff. She wanted him to just turn and go up the three steps to her back porch, go on in ahead of her. She didn't want to have to approach him, to move past him, to lead the way, with him at her back, watching.

But of course, he wouldn't go ahead of her. It was her house, her responsibility to show a first-time guest inside.

"Well," she said, and forced her feet to move.

Neither of them seemed capable of looking away. She advanced and he just stood there. And then, when she came even with him, she closed her eyes, briefly, breaking the hold of his gaze. She moved by, went up the steps. He followed. His tread was light, but she felt every footfall, pressing on her, in some deep, private place. She paused to pick up her basket of tomatoes, to drop her gloves at the edge of the step. Then she went on, pulling open the door and standing back.

He went in, and she followed, onto the service porch where her washer and dryer and laundry supplies lined one wall and her bucket of dirty carrots waited on the edge of the doormat to be cleaned.

The porch half bath was through the door to her right. She wanted to go in there, rinse off her sweating face, run a comb through her hair. But no. Not right now, not with him standing here, waiting. Better to show him on in first.

She had dirt on her shoes. "Hold on a second..."

He said nothing, just stood to the side a little and watched as she set down the tomatoes, shucked off her gardening clogs, got rid of her slightly grimy socks, tossing them in the wicker laundry basket on top of the dryer. Her pale feet seemed very bare—defenseless, without her socks. A few evenings ago, she'd given herself a long, lovely pedicure, buffing and pumicing and stroking clear polish on her toenails at the end.

She despised herself right now because she was glad that she had.

Swiftly she slipped on a pair of sandals and picked up the basket again. "Okay." Her voice was absurdly breathy and urgent. "This way." She moved ahead

again, opened the inner door and went through. He
followed.

They entered what she thought of as the family
room. Bookshelves lined the walls, the blind eye of
a television stared from a corner and the furniture was
a little bit worn and very comfortable. She took him
through the open doorway to the kitchen and gestured
at the bay window and the round oak table in front
of it. "Make yourself comfortable." She set the tomatoes on the counter. "And if you'd give me one
minute?"

"Sure."

She retraced her steps, through the family room and
out to the service porch, then on into the half bath at
last. She shut the door, rested her head against the
wood, closed her eyes and let out a long, shaky sigh.
Then she drew herself up and turned to face the mirror above the sink.

Her eyes were wide, haunted-looking. Twin spots
of hectic color stained her cheeks.

This was awful, impossible, wrong. Had she
learned nothing from the mess she'd made of her life
once? It certainly didn't feel like it, not with the way
her heart was pounding, the way she burned with hungry heat.

She might as well have been seventeen again, that
first time she snuck Rusty into her parents' house.
Seventeen, with her parents gone—off somewhere.
She couldn't remember where, but it would have been
two separate places. Her mom and dad didn't go out
together much. But wherever they were, neither of
them had a clue what their bright, perfect, well-

behaved daughter was up to. That she had Rusty in the house.

Yes. She had Rusty in the house and she knew that he was going to kiss her. And she knew that he wouldn't stop with just kisses.

And she was glad.

"Oh, God," she whispered low.

She flipped on the cold tap and splashed water on her face, grabbing the hand towel, scrubbing at her cheeks as if she could wipe away not only the water, but the heat in them, the evidence of her own insistent, self-destructive attraction to the wrong kind of man. She got a brush from the drawer and tugged it angrily through her hair, trying to tame it. Failing that, she found a scrunchy in the other drawer and anchored the mess in a ponytail, low on her neck.

"There," she whispered to her reflection, "Better. Really. It's really okay." Swiftly she tucked her raggedy shirt more securely into the waistband of her baggy old jeans.

And then there was nothing else to do but get out there and deal with him.

He was sitting at the table when she reentered the kitchen, but he'd turned his chair out a little, so he could comfortably face the doorway to the family room. He wore faded denim and worn tan boots and his skin looked golden in contrast to his white T-shirt. He was Brad Pitt in *Fight Club,* Ben Affleck out of rehab. He was a young Paul Newman in that old Faulkner movie, *The Long Hot Summer,* the barn burner's son looking for more than any woman ought to give him. He was sin just waiting to happen.

And *why,* she found herself wondering? *Why me?*

What did he see in her? Not that there was anything *wrong* with her, just that she simply was not his type. Not gorgeous, not glamorous, not a party animal.

And look at her wardrobe. Eddie Bauer and L.L. Bean—and, times like right now, when she'd been gardening, various little numbers one step away from the ragbag. Cade Bravo's women wore DKNY and Versace. They probably all bought their underwear at Victoria's Secret.

It made no sense. No sense at all.

But then, it had been the same with Rusty. Attraction of opposites. A good girl and a bad boy, tasting the forbidden, doing what they shouldn't do.

And loving every minute of it.

At least, for a while.

"Iced tea, you said?"

"Great."

"Sugar? Lemon?"

"Plain."

Her refrigerator had an ice maker in the freezer door. She got a pair of glasses from the cupboard and stuck them under the ice dispenser, one and then the other. The cubes dropping into place sounded like gunshots in the too-quiet room.

She got out the tea, poured it over the ice, filling both glasses. Normally she liked sugar and lemon. But no way she was fooling with any of that right now.

She put the tea away, picked up the two glasses and carried them to the table, setting his in front of him, then sliding into a chair.

"Thanks," he said.

She gave him a tight smile and a nod in response. Then, not knowing what else to do, she sipped from her tea—too bitter, not tart enough.

She set it down in front of her and looked at it. She was afraid to look anywhere else, and that was a plain fact.

"Jane."

He was waiting, she knew. For her to look at him.

Better get it over with. She dragged her gaze upward, and she met those silver eyes again.

And he said it. "I want to go out with you. Dinner. A show. It doesn't matter to me. Whatever you want, that's what we'll do."

She looked at him, into those eyes. "Thank you. For asking me." The words came out flat, without intonation. "I'm sorry. But no. I can't go out with you."

He didn't look surprised. "Can't?" He was mocking her.

She couldn't blame him for his scorn. *Can't,* in this case, was a coward's word. And a lie. "I won't. I won't go out with you."

"Why not?"

She shut her eyes, dragged in a long breath, then looked at him again. "Won't you just take what I said? Take *no thank you,* and let it be?"

He smiled then, more or less. At least the corners of his mouth hitched upward. "I will, if that's all I can get. It's not like I really have a choice. But you're honest, or you try to be, and—"

"How do you know that?"

"Does it matter?"

It did matter, a lot, for some reason. "I'd like to know how you know that about me, that's all."

"Jane. How could I not know?"

"You mean you've been watching me."

"What? That's news? It offends you, that I like to look at you, that I listen when people talk about you?"

"Who? Who talks about me?"

"Oh, come on. Your buddy Celia's married to Aaron. It's a story she likes to tell, how she fell in love with my brother and you told her to be honest, to let him know how she felt, that honesty was always the best policy. Is that right? Did that happen?"

She nodded, feeling vaguely foolish for making a big deal out of not very much. "Yes. All right. It happened."

"And your other friend, Jillian, she said Celia should wear sexier clothes and brighter colors, make him notice her as a woman first before she told him she was gone on him."

Jane couldn't help smiling at the memory. "And Celia did both—told the truth *and* bought a few new clothes."

"Yeah. And look at them now."

"Yes," she said carefully. "They're very happy." They lived in Las Vegas. Aaron was part owner and CEO of High Sierra Resort and Casino, on the Strip. Celia was his secretary and personal assistant—and now, his wife as well.

Cade said, "And I haven't forgotten what I asked in the first place. Did you think I would?"

Yes. All right. Maybe she had. She regarded him warily, her mouth firmly shut.

He asked again, "Why won't you go out with me?"

Jane looked through the bay window at her backyard, wishing she was out there, deadheading mums and geraniums, digging up more dandelions, working that long, tenacious central root up out of the soil. Anything but this, having to tell this man *no* when her body and her wayward heart wouldn't stop crying *yes.*

"Well?" he prompted.

She looked at him again and she spoke with defiance. "You know why. You're from town. You know about me. I had a bad marriage. A really bad marriage."

"I didn't mention marriage, Jane."

"Well, of course you didn't."

"Did you want me to?"

"Did you plan to?"

He grunted. "No. As a matter of fact, marriage wasn't what I had in mind."

"Exactly. And that's another reason for me *not* to go out with you. We want completely different things from a relationship."

"Do we?" His eyes said things she shouldn't let herself hear.

"Nothing is going to happen between us," she said, slowly. Firmly. With much more conviction than she actually felt. "What I want from a relationship, you're not willing to give."

He lifted an eyebrow at her. "You're saying you want to get married again?"

"Yes, I do. And I want a *good* marriage this time. When it comes to a man, I'm looking for an equal— an equal and a best friend."

That fine mouth curved, ever so slightly, in another one of those almost-smiles. "Well, all right. Let's be friends."

She did not smile back, not even marginally. "You're not taking me seriously."

"Yes, I am. You want a man to be your friend. Fine. Let's be friends."

It was a trap. She knew it. They'd play at being friends. And eventually, they'd make each other crazy enough that they'd give in to what was really driving this. And she should be insulted, that he would sit here in her kitchen and pretend to offer friendship when they both knew what he really wanted from her.

But she wasn't insulted. She was too excited to be insulted. She just wanted to say yes—Yes, yes, *yes*. Whatever he wanted, however he wanted it.

"No." She had to push the word out of her mouth. "I won't be your friend."

His long hand cupped his glass of tea. He stroked, wiping the moisture clinging to the side of the glass, so it slid down and pooled on the table. "Why not?"

She looked away from that stroking hand, made a low, tight sound of disbelief. "Because I really don't think that my friendship is what you're after."

She was looking at his hand again. Slowly he turned the glass in a circle, smearing the puddle of moisture at the base of it. "You don't, huh?"

She yanked her gaze upward and glared at him. "No, I don't. Are you going to tell me I've got it all wrong?"

There it was again, the smile that didn't quite happen. "Let me put it this way. I'll try anything once, friendship included."

She felt vaguely ridiculous, to keep on with this, to make all this effort to be truthful when she didn't *feel* truthful, when she knew he was teasing her, making fun of what she said. But she did keep on. Because however pointless it felt to tell him these things, she believed they were things that had to be said. "I want marriage, a good marriage. I want a steady man, a man who'll stick by me, a man who'll be true."

He had that golden head tipped to the side, as if he were considering whether or not to say what was in his mind.

"What?" she demanded. "Just say it. Say it now."

He lifted one hard shoulder in a shrug. "Okay. How long's it been, since Rusty died? You were, what, twenty?"

She had to clear her throat before she could answer. "Twenty-one. It's been six years."

"You run into any steady men, since then? Any true, good men?"

"Yes. Yes, of course, I have."

"You dated a few of them, of those good guys, those solid guys?"

"That's right. I did."

"So what happened? How come you're not with one of them now?"

Silently she cursed him. For knowing her secret

truth, for hitting it right on the mark. "It didn't work out, that's all."

"You're looking away again. Let's have some truth, Jane. Let's have it out straight."

She snapped her gaze back to collide with his and she muttered between clenched teeth, "You're being purposely cruel. I've had enough of that, in my life. Cruelty. From a man."

He leaned her way, just a little, enough that she felt him, encroaching, not quite enough to make her move back. "Listen," he said in a low voice. "I'm not him. Not Rusty. Yeah, all right, I've had my run-ins with the law. I've made trouble. I'm not exactly a solid citizen. And I've got no interest in getting married. But I've never held up a damn convenience store. I earn my way. I pay for what's mine. And the kind of cruel I'm guessing Rusty Jenkins was to you, I'm not and would never be. Get out your stack of bibles. I can swear to that."

Her lips felt dry and hot. She licked them.

His gaze flicked down, watched her do that. "God," he whispered.

And she forgot everything, but the sound of his voice and the shape of his mouth. All at once, they were leaning in, both of them. She smelled him, smelled the heat and the maleness, the clean cotton scent of his T-shirt. She felt his breath across her cheek.

Just before their lips could meet, she shoved her chair back and jumped to her feet. "No." It came out every bit as desperate-sounding as she felt. "No, please…"

He sat back, draping a hard arm over the back of the chair, looking up at her through lazy, knowing eyes. "I wasn't sure. About you, about how you felt. Sometimes, when a man wants a woman, it's easy to imagine reactions that aren't really there. But it's there, isn't it? It's as bad for you as it is for me."

She clenched her fists at her sides. What could she say to that? What could she tell him? The truth was unacceptable. And she was not a woman who told lies. "Nothing is going to happen between us. It's...not what I want. Please understand."

"Not what you want?"

"You know what I mean."

"Oh, yeah. I think I do." The gleam in those pale eyes told it all. He knew what she meant, all right. All the *wrong* things she meant. Her good intentions were nothing to him.

"You're purposely misconstruing what I'm saying."

"You're not saying what you really mean."

"I am. Yes. I'm not going to go out with you. Nothing is going to happen between us. You'd better forget me. And I'll forget you."

He shook his head. That smile that wasn't quite a smile was back on his sinfully beautiful face. "How long's it been, since this started, this thing between us, this thing that you keep telling yourself is going to just fade away? Months, anyway, right?"

"What does it matter? I want you to go now."

He didn't budge from that chair. "It matters because you've been fighting it, right? And don't think I haven't been fighting it, too. I have. I mean, come on, I got your messages. Loud and clear. You know the ones. *Get back. Keep away. Don't come near.*"

"But here you are, anyway." She was sneering. She couldn't seem to stop herself. "Sitting in my kitchen."

"You invited me in."

"And I also asked you to leave, not two minutes ago."

He chuckled then. "Jane, Jane, Jane…"

"Stop that!" She realized she'd shouted, brought the volume down to a whisper of rage. "Don't you laugh at me."

His face had gone dead serious. "I'm not. You know I'm not. I'm just telling you the truth. Being honest, the way you say you want it. I don't think this is funny at all. The truth is, I want you. You want me. You deny it. I deny it. But it keeps on. It's kept on for months. Ignoring it is not going to make it go away."

She had no reply for that. He was right. They both knew it. "Look. I mean it. I'd like you to leave now."

"Fine." He gathered those long legs up and stood.

She stepped back, clear of him. His body could not be allowed to touch hers—even accidentally, in passing.

He gave her a look that burned and chilled at the same time. "I suppose you want me to go out like I came in. Through the back. That way, there's less chance someone might see that I was in here, less chance your mother might hear about it."

She drew herself up. "The implication being that my mother somehow runs my life?"

"Admit it." His voice was way too soft. "You don't want her to know I was here."

It was Jane's turn to shrug. "Okay. It would make it easier on me if she didn't know—which is a very good reason for you to go out the front."

He frowned. "I don't get it."

"I invited you in here. I'm not ashamed that I did. If my mother finds out, well, okay. She finds out."

"She hates me—hates all us bad Bravos. You know that, don't you?"

She did. "My mother is difficult. Her life didn't work out the way she would have liked it to. She has a tendency to take out her disappointments on others. It's sad, really. She needs love so much, yet she's always pushing people away."

He wore a musing look. "You surprise me."

"Because I know my own mother?"

"I guess. I had you pegged differently, when it came to her."

"Maybe you had me pegged wrong."

"Maybe so."

"The point is, I'm a grown woman. I've done nothing wrong here. Neither of us has. And I won't live like a guilty child."

He studied her for a moment, then he let out a hard breath. "Whatever. But I still think it's best if I just leave through the back." He started to move past her.

"Wait." She reached out. He froze, his eyes daring her. She continued the movement, lifting her reaching hand to smooth her hair. The gesture didn't fool either of them. She had almost touched him, had stopped herself just in time.

She dropped her hand. "This way."

"Hey. Relax."

"You'll go out the front."

He seemed amused. "Is that an order?"

"Just a statement of fact."

"Okay, no problem. I can find the door myself."

"No. I will see you out."

He looked her up and down, his gaze sparking heat everywhere it touched. "So damn well brought up, aren't you, Jane?"

Was that supposed to be an insult? "Yes, I am."

She turned for the open doorway, but instead of going straight, into the family room, she went left, entering the central hall. He came along behind. It seemed to take a very long time to reach the front door.

But at last, they were there. She grabbed the door handle and pulled the door wide, unlatching the screen, pushing it open. He went through, out onto her porch, down the steps, into the sun that found the gold in his silky hair and reflected off his white T-shirt, so that she blinked against the sudden blinding brightness of just looking at him.

At the bottom of the steps, he paused and turned to her. "Thanks. For the iced tea."

He hadn't taken so much as a sip. "You're welcome."

"I'll have to think about this. What you said. What you meant."

"Don't. Please. Just let it go."

He looked her up and down again, as he had done back in the kitchen, slowly, assessingly, causing heat to flare and flash and pop along the surface of her skin, making that heaviness down in the center of her, that willingness in spite of her wiser self.

"You probably shouldn't have invited me in."

It had seemed the decent thing to do. "Maybe not," she confessed.

He turned, took a few more steps, then turned again, so he was walking backward away from her, not quite smiling, in that way of his. Her heart lifted. For a fraction of a second, he was only a man she found attractive, walking away from her, but reluctant to go.

"Pretty," he said, reaching out his left hand, brushing the surface of one of the gleaming glass spheres tucked among the cosmos. The gold bracelet he always wore caught the sunlight and winked at her.

She smiled at him.

He saluted her, the way he had that morning, two fingers briefly touching his forehead. Then he turned toward the street again and continued down the walk.

She closed the screen and shut the door and told herself that whatever he hinted at, nothing would happen. She'd ended it before it had a chance to begin.

Chapter Four

Cade left town sometime the next day.

When Jane got home from the bookstore Monday night, his house was dark. The green Porsche was nowhere in sight. At a little after noon, on Tuesday, Jane spotted Caitlin on Cade's porch, picking up the mail and papers as she always did whenever he went away.

Wednesday, at a little before five, Gary Nevis dropped in at her store. He bought a book on western wildflowers and asked her to have dinner with him Saturday night.

She looked into his handsome, friendly face and felt like crying. He was just what she was looking for. Except for one little problem. He didn't fill her fantasies.

And he never would. That *thing,* that spark, that whatever-it-was. With Gary, well, it just wasn't there.

In the back of her mind, Cade's taunts echoed, *You run into any steady men, any true, good men? You dated a few of them, those good guys, those solid guys? So what happened? How come you're not with one of them now?*

She turned Gary down, softly and firmly. She could see in his eyes that he understood the extent of her refusal. He wouldn't be asking again.

She'd already been feeling low. After that, she felt lower still.

She arrived home at a little after nine that night. The house next door remained dark. No green Porsche crouched at the curb.

Jane went to bed around ten, drifted off to sleep and then woke at a little after three. She lay there, staring into the darkness, until she couldn't bear it for another second. Finally she gave in. She got up and looked out the window.

Big surprise. His house was dark. She went back to her bed and turned her pillow over to the cool side. She punched it to fluff it a little. Then she resolutely closed her eyes.

Sleep was a long time coming. Sometimes her mind could be every bit as unruly as her hair.

Thursday at four Jane held her biweekly Children's Story Hour. She had a presentation area in the rear of the store, with a mishmash of chairs and benches— and also with a lot of plump pillows in the corners for folks who preferred to sit on the floor. She held the story hour there, as she did the various readers' groups she hosted, the occasional musical evening and any speaker or workshop events.

As it turned out, the story hour was just what she needed. She read some Dr. Seuss and a little Shel Silverstein and then a few chapters from *Charlie and the Chocolate Factory.*

Her heart lifted as she looked out over the small, wide-eyed faces, and she felt a smile breaking through the gloom that had been dogging her since she told two men no—one she wanted and one she didn't, one who was all wrong and one who was just right. Reading to the kids always raised her spirits, brought hope to life again.

Someday, she *would* find the right guy. She would marry again, this time well and wisely, marry a man who not only turned her bones to water, but who also loved and respected her, a man who would never hurt her, a man who wanted children as much as she did.

Jillian Diamond came bouncing into the bookstore at a little after six on Friday.

Jillian had her own business, Image by Jillian. She taught her clients how to dress for success. She also wrote a column, "Ask Jillian," for the *Sacramento Press-Telegram.* She'd already spoken at Jane's store once, back in March. Lots of folks showed up and Jillian had really wowed them. She was funny and she had some quirky and fascinating ideas. Jane had prevailed on her to do it again.

For her talk this time, Jillian wore a short, sleeveless, fitted sheath in a geometric print and a pair of white patent go-go boots. Her gold-streaked brown hair curled loosely around her arresting face. Her gray eyes sparkled beneath those startlingly dark, thick brows.

"Janey, I made it. Have to tell you, though, I had my doubts. What is it with Highway 50, anyway? Is there ever a time when half the lanes aren't blocked off for repairs?"

"Sure. That would be in the middle of winter, when *all* the lanes are closed due to ice and snow." They hugged.

Jillian smelled of her favorite perfume, Ralph Lauren's Romance, and also of Cheez Doodles. She was carrying an open bag of them. She stepped back from the hug and popped one in her mouth, then held out the bag to Jane.

"No, thanks."

"I stopped by the house and left my suitcase and stuff." Jillian gobbled more Cheez Doodles. Jane wondered how she did it. Jillian ate whatever she wanted and she never worked out and she weighed just what she'd weighed the day they graduated from New Venice High—which was about one-fifteen, soaking wet. In go-go boots.

"Oh, I am starving," said Jillian. "And I'm in a burger kind of mood. Let's go next door."

Next door. To Caitlin Bravo's place.

"To the Highgrade?" It came out sounding grim, though Jane truly hadn't meant it that way. Really, there was no reason to avoid the place. Cade wouldn't be there. He wasn't even in town.

"Janey. Sometimes you are a total food snob."

"I am not. I love a good burger as much as any-body."

"Then what is the hang-up here?" Jillian slid a glance at Madelyn, Jane's clerk, who was busy ring-ing up a sale at the register. Then she leaned close and whispered, "A Mommy Dearest issue?"

"No, nothing like that." Until the day Jane turned eighteen and eloped with Rusty, thus declaring her independence from Virginia Elliott in a very big way, she never would have dared to upset her mother by entering Caitlin Bravo's place of business. But all that was years ago. Now, Jane ran her own life and al-lowed no one to tell her where she could or couldn't go. She often headed over to the café next door for a sandwich—or she used to, until recently, when she'd become increasingly worried she might run into Cade there.

Jillian's thick brows were all scrunched up. "Well if there are no, er, family issues involved and you love burgers, why not?"

"Good question." Jane tried to sound breezy. "If you want to eat there, it's fine with me."

Jillian stepped up to the register and offered the rest of her Cheez Doodles to Madelyn. "Enjoy." She brushed the orange dust from her hands and turned back to Jane. "Let's go."

Caitlin was there to greet them. "Well, look who's here." She emerged from behind the cash register counter in the Highgrade's central game room. "What's up?"

Jillian told her. "I'm speaking next-door at Jane's tonight."

"Speaking of what?"

"*Having It All and Loving It. How to Please Both Yourself* and *Your Man.*"

Caitlin chuckled her low, naughty-sounding chuckle. "Well. I'd say that about covers everything."

"Drop over if you get a chance."

"Sweetie, I just might take you up on that—and right now, I suppose you two want to eat?"

"You bet." Jillian's eyes were shining. "I'm starved. For a bacon and Swiss burger, I think. With onion rings and a chocolate shake—but I'll have a look at the menu, just in case something else jumps out at me."

Caitlin's false eyelashes swept down. When she looked up again, it was straight at Jane. "We've missed you around here lately."

"Oh, well, things have been really busy."

"I'm still counting on you to do your story lady gig at the picnic Labor Day." The Labor Day picnic was an annual event in New Venice. The town merchants went all out for it. There were horseshoes and shuffleboard, live bands, beer on tap for the grownups, a clown show and face-painting booth for the kids—among other things. Caitlin was heading up the picnic committee this year.

"I'm looking forward to it."

"Good. And don't be a damn stranger. You can drop in for a sandwich anytime and be back at your store in twenty minutes flat. I will personally expedite your order.''

"Thank you. I'll remember that.''

"Don't thank me. Just come around more often.''

"Yes. I will. Honestly.''

"This way.'' Caitlin led them through the open doorway to the café and straight to a corner booth. She gestured at the big laminated menus, which were tucked upright between the sugar dispenser and the napkin holder. "Have a look.'' The orange sequins on her tight black shirt glittered aggressively with every breath she took. "I'll send Roxy right over.'' She strutted off.

Jillian picked up her menu and spoke from behind it, out of the corner of her mouth. "God. Best butt I've ever seen on a woman over forty-five.''

Jane whispered back. "She is one of a kind.''

"And I swear, she's a 38-D. Just like you. And not saggy, either.''

"Fascinating,'' said Jane dryly. "What are you having?''

"I'm looking, I'm looking….''

"Right.'' Jane studied her menu, which had a knotty-pine fence on the cover—no doubt to go along with the Highgrade's extensively knotty-pine decor. Inside, a cartoon miner with a big hat, baggy old jeans and a pickax slung over his shoulder, grinned and pointed at the various menu selections. "The club sandwich is always good.''

Jillian wasn't listening—or looking at the menu. "I don't see the Viking Hunk.'' The Viking Hunk was Caitlin's on-again, off-again lover, Hans. He was about Cade's age, had long blond hair and looked like he'd walked right off the cover of a steamy romance novel.

Jane shrugged. "You're right. Hans hasn't been around lately. I think I heard he's left town again."

"Ah, the course of true love never did run all that smooth."

"Here comes the waitress. Quit mangling Shakespeare and figure out what you want."

They ordered and the food arrived quickly. Jane concentrated on her sandwich and tried not to remember….

That engagement party Caitlin had thrown here for Aaron and Celia back at the beginning of May. The place had been packed for that. There had even been other Bravos, specifically the famous Bravo billionaire, Jonas, from Los Angeles, and his wife, Emma. Jonas was Cade's cousin and his presence had surprised every one. For over thirty years, Caitlin and her sons had lived as if no other Bravos existed. But Celia—and Jonas's wife, Emma—were working to change all that.

"Hey, Jane." Cade's voice had come from behind her. It was friendly, slightly teasing, nothing in the least pushy about it. Still, she felt pushed, way down inside herself. Pushed and pulled at the same time.

She'd turned and put on a smile. "Hello, Cade. How are you?"

"Doin' okay. Did you eat yet? I was just going to go and fill myself a plate."

"Thanks, but I'm not all that hungry right now."

*Those strange, beautiful eyes went from molten sil-
ver to ice. "Right. Not hungry."*

*She spotted her excuse to escape him on the other
side of the room. "Oh, there's Jilly. I've been looking
for her..." She left him, weaving her way quickly
through the press of people, a slight shudder moving
through her at the thought that might follow her, perhaps become more insistent....*

But he didn't.

*And then, a few weeks ago—she'd seen him in here
again. He'd been in the game room, kind of lounging
against the wall, chatting with Donny Verdun, who
ran the convenience store at the corner of State and
Main. She'd tried to slide on into the café without
him spotting her.*

But no such luck.

*Two minutes after she sat down, there he was,
standing by her booth, asking her how she'd been
doing, those eyes of his looking into hers, telling her
things his mouth wouldn't dare say.*

*She'd come very close to rudeness that time, in-
sisting she was in a hurry. Could he please send the
waitress over right away?*

"Sure, Jane. I'll do that." And he was gone.

She'd felt small and mean then—and strangely be-
reft. After that, she'd decided maybe it would be better if she stopped eating at the Highgrade for a while.

"Yoo-hoo, Janey. Are you there?"

She blinked and looked down at her hands. At
some point, she had picked up the tube of paper that
had covered her straw. She was wrapping it absent-
mindedly around her index finger. "What?" She

yanked off the flattened tube of paper and dropped it on her plate beside her half-eaten club sandwich.

"You should see your face. Dreamy." Jillian set down her milkshake and leaned in close. "There's someone, isn't there? At last, after all these years. Come on. Tell Jillian. Who is he?"

"Oh, Jilly. Eat your Swiss and bacon burger. We can't sit here all night."

Later, back at the bookstore, Jane kept half expecting Caitlin to walk in. But she never appeared.

Jane closed up at ten. She'd walked to the store that morning. Since Jillian, who never walked anywhere if she could help it, had driven over from the house in the afternoon, Jane rode home with her.

They stayed up till a little before two, drinking wine at first and then switching to herbal tea around midnight.

They talked about the things they always talked about. The bookstore. Jillian's career. Celia.

"I called her last Saturday," Jane reported. "She sounded great. I forgot to ask her about the Labor Day picnic, though."

"Where you are playing story lady, right?"

"Right. I know Aaron's helping out, hiring the bands for it. But I still don't know if he and Celia are planning to be here for it—and how about you? Will you come this year?"

"Yeah. I could probably be here. I'll let you know."

The next morning, Jillian slept in.

Jane had to open the store at ten, so she was up at

eight. She sat at her kitchen table with the morning sun pouring in the bay window and sipped her coffee and told herself that life was good.

And maybe Cade would stay away for weeks this time, the way he used to, back before his house was finished.

She smiled a sad little smile and sipped more coffee. Yes, that would be good for her. It really would. But whether he stayed away or not, she would get over this impossible, unhealthy attraction. No doubt about it. It was only a matter of time.

Jillian left early Sunday morning.

And Jane's mother called. "Hi, dear. How about church?"

"I'd love it."

"Why don't we just meet there?" Virginia suggested. "I'm running a little late."

When Jane left the house, she saw Cade's powerful green car parked at the curb next door.

He was back.

Her heart felt like something was squeezing it. Then it started beating way too fast.

Get over it, she told herself as she got in her van and started it up. *He lives here and he's going to be here a lot of the time. Accept it.*

And forget him.

"How about a sandwich and some iced tea at my house?" Jane offered, as she and Virginia walked down the church steps toward the cars waiting at the curb.

"Wonderful," said Virginia.

Her mother followed her home.

The first thing Jane noticed when she turned onto her street was that the green Porsche was gone again. Good. She got out of her van and waited for Virginia to park.

They started up the walk together.

Jane saw the object on the porch—on the mat, right in front of the door—at about the same time her mother did.

"Jane. What *is* that?"

Jane didn't answer. She walked a little faster. Soon enough, they both stood on the porch, looking down at it.

Virginia said, "Why, it's so beautiful. It looks like an antique."

"It is an antique," Jane said softly, staring down at the gorgeous thing. "I'm almost certain of it. An antique mercury glass gazing ball and vase, in one." The silvery-gold ball sat on a central glass platform, with a clever little trough all around it where the flowers would go.

"A gazing ball? Like the ones in your garden?"

"Not quite," Jane said dryly. "My guess is that this is the real thing."

"The real thing. How so?"

Jane gestured toward the gazing balls that gleamed among the cosmos along her front walk. "Those you can find in just about any garden shop. They're made of a single layer of glass treated with some sort of transparent opalescent paint."

"And this?"

"It's an old technique. They would flow real mercury between two layers of glass. They don't make them like that anymore, though. They haven't in decades." Jane had read about such treasures in the various books on rare glassware she kept in her store. She couldn't resist. She had to know for certain. "Here. Hold these a minute, will you?" She handed her mother her keys and her small purse. Then she knelt and oh-so-carefully slipped her fingers beneath the vase.

"Yes." She grinned.

"Yes, *what?*" Virginia demanded.

"I can feel the stopper underneath. They would have to use a stopper, to hold in the mercury." She lifted it. "And it's heavy. Mercury is heavy. That means it still has its original filling."

Her mother was frowning at her. "It's filled with real mercury?"

"That's right. And that's very rare. Most of the old pieces like this have been drained, with reflective paint injected in the mercury's place."

"Better not drop it," her mother said warily. "Just what we need. Mercury all over the place."

"I'm not going to drop it." So beautiful, Jane thought. She stood again, carefully, cradling the precious vase close to her body.

"Who could have left it here, do you think?" Virginia was intrigued—and suspicious, too.

Jane shrugged and made a noncommittal noise, evading her mother's question, coming perilously close to telling a lie.

Because she knew very well who had left it there.

If she closed her eyes, she could see him now, walking backward down the walk, the sun gleaming golden in his hair, reaching out to brush those long fingers across one of the shining globes tucked among the flowers.

"Jane?" her mother prompted. "I asked who would leave something like this on your front porch."

Jane considered telling her mother the truth. But it would only be inviting more questions—not to mention an excess of outraged noises at the very idea that Cade Bravo would dare to offer expensive gifts to Virginia Elliott's only daughter.

She settled for shrugging again. "Open the door, Mom. Let's go inside and I'll make our lunch."

Chapter Five

Jane set the golden vase carefully on the narrow table near the front door.

"It must be valuable," Virginia said.

"Yes, I'm sure it is."

They both stood back for a moment, admiring it. It reflected light so beautifully, with the shiny golden surface—veined in places, after years and years—and that layer of quicksilver trapped beneath. It seemed almost magical, managing somehow to be opaque *and* transparent *and* reflecting all at once. It was all curves, too, distorting in a fascinating way what it mirrored, so that, staring into it, Jane's entry hall became a strange and fantastical otherworldly place.

"And you don't know who left it on the front mat?" Her mother sent her a quizzing, narrow-eyed look.

Jane made another noncommittal sound.

"That means you know, but you're not telling," said Virginia, her tone accusing now.

Jane gave her mother a smile. "Lunch will only take a few minutes. Let's go on in the kitchen."

They ate at the oak table by the bay window. Twice more, Virginia tried to pry from her daughter the name of the person Jane believed had left the vase. Finally Jane decided she'd had enough.

"Mom, by now you must have gotten the message that I don't want to go into this. I'd appreciate it if you'd just leave the subject alone."

"Well, but why wouldn't you want to talk about it? It makes no sense that you'd be so touchy about something like this."

"If I'm touchy, it's because I've asked you to let the subject drop—and you haven't."

"But—" Virginia began, and then had the grace to cut herself off. She shook her head and conceded in a thoroughly wounded tone, "Well, all right. I won't say another word about it."

"Thank you. More iced tea?"

"Yes. I suppose. One more glass."

Virginia left about a half hour later, with a bouquet of blood-red roses and three grocery bags, one each of tomatoes, string beans and zucchini. Jane felt marginally guilty loading her poor mother up with all those vegetables. There were only the two of them, her mother and her father, at home now, after all. And her father rarely showed up to sit down to dinner with his wife.

Clifford Elliott was district judge and he sat on the

boards of various trusts and charities. And then there were all the organizations he belonged to, the Masons and the Knights of Columbus, to name just two. Both he and Virginia liked to say that he "kept very busy." The fact that he was away so much and didn't share his wife's bed when he finally did come home was one of those things that simply wasn't talked about.

Virginia said, "Belinda's coming Wednesday." Belinda was her housekeeper. "I can share some of these beautiful vegetables with her. And I'll make some zucchini bread. It freezes well." Jane helped her mother carry it all out to the car.

The Porsche was back again. Cade must be home. Good. She had a thing or two to say to him. She kissed her mother's cheek and stood waving as Virginia drove off.

Once the Lincoln turned the corner, Jane headed for her house again. She marched up the walk, mounted the steps and went inside. The outer door closed automatically behind her.

Leaving the heavy oak inner door standing open, she went for the vase, which gleamed, breathtakingly beautiful, on her entry hall table to the right of the door. She paused, caught again by the absolute perfection of it as a gift meant specifically for her, for Jane Elizabeth Elliott.

She knew a sharp pang of regret. She wanted to keep it. A lot.

But she couldn't keep it. And she knew it.

Gathering it gently into her arms, surprised anew at its weight, she turned for the door again and circled back around it, cradling the vase with great care. She planned to ease through the screen with a nudge of her shoulder.

What she hadn't planned on was Cade.

He was there, standing on her welcome mat, looking at her through the screened top half of the outer door, holding an enormous bouquet of bright yellow daisies.

She gasped and almost dropped the vase.

And he grinned.

She could have shot him. Luckily for both of them, she didn't own a gun. She glared at him through the screen.

"Hello, Jane."

She said nothing, simply turned again and retraced her steps around the door. Carefully she slid her burden back onto the narrow table, breathing a sigh of relief to have it out of her arms and in a place of relative safety once more.

He was still waiting. He had to be dealt with. She smoothed her hands down the front of the sleeveless linen dress she wore, half hoping he might just turn around and leave, knowing at the same time that if he did, she'd only end up having to go after him. She had to confront him and she knew it. She must return his gift and make it clear, once again, that whatever ideas he had in his mind about her, he might as well give them up, because ideas were all they would ever be.

She forced her feet to move, around the open door again, into the doorway behind the screen. "I was just coming over to talk to you."

He looked at her, a long look, a look that blasted

her defenses, a look that stripped her down to flesh and sensation and the longings she kept trying so valiantly to deny. "You plan to let me in?"

The word *no* did occur to her. But she didn't say it. Instead she pushed on the screen. He stepped back, until she had it all the way open. Then, just like last Sunday, he was inside.

He held out the daisies. "I know you've got all the flowers you need. But I wanted to get you some anyway. It seemed only right to get them to go with the vase."

He looked so tender. So hopeful. So infinitely woundable. And she'd always had a weakness for daisies....

She stepped back, put out both hands in a warding-off gesture. "I can't take them. You know that. And I can't take the vase."

He gave her another of those long, assessing, knee-weakening looks of his. She clutched desperately for all the reasons she could never, ever go out with him, reminded herself frantically, *This is the guy that Rusty used to idolize.*

She could almost hear Rusty's voice now. "Man, that Cade Bravo. Did you hear the latest? Your uncle locked him up again this week—for being drunk and disorderly." Or "Cade Bravo got picked up for speeding. He was drunk, too, from what I heard. Got himself another DUI. He told old J.T. off, too. No one tells Cade Bravo what to do...."

Once, on a dare, Cade had run down Main Street naked. Nobody in town had ever forgotten that, the day Cade Bravo streaked Main.

And then there were all the women. Cade had always had a way with the women. People whispered that he had got Enda Cheevers pregnant, back when he and Enda were both in high school, and then refused to marry her even when Enda's father came after him with a shotgun. And another girl, Desiree Lott, had carved his name on her forehead with a pocketknife to prove her love for him. The story went that Cade had told her she was crazy and then refused to go out with her again. Desiree had a breakdown and had to be sent away.

And then, as he got well into his twenties and no longer lived in town, he'd return now and then with some new, drop-dead gorgeous woman on his arm. Never, that Jane knew of, had he brought the same woman home twice.

He was not, by any stretch of a vivid imagination, the kind of man she was looking for. She had to remember that.

She had to stay strong against his tender, I-am-so-vulnerable looks, his for-her-and-her-alone gifts. Of course, he would have the tender looks down pat. And he would know the ways to please a woman, know just what to do to get a woman to want him.

He ought to know. After all, he'd had enough practice at it.

Cade turned and set the flowers on the hall table, a few inches from the vase.

"Cade," she said to the back of his golden head. "I am serious. I told you, last Sunday, how I felt. I told you—"

He turned on her then, a seamless, catlike movement. "No." Those silver eyes burned through her. "You didn't say how you felt. You didn't say how you felt at all."

"All right. Maybe I put that wrong."

"Oh, I don't think so."

"Listen. Whatever I might have felt, I did say *no*. I said—"

"I remember. You said nothing would be happening between us."

"That's right. And I said it more than once, too."

"Yeah, Jane. You did."

"Then if you know that, if you admit you remember my telling you that—"

"What?" he demanded.

So she told him what. "Why are you here? What are you up to? Leaving presents, *expensive* presents, on my doorstep while I'm away at church, so I can find them when I come home, with my *mother*—and don't tell me you didn't realize that, didn't know that my mother would be right beside me when I found that vase."

"Wait a minute." He was shaking his head. "No. No, I didn't know your mother would be with you when you got back home."

"Oh, please. You know very well that I go to church with her most Sundays. And you also know how my mother feels about you. So you must have thoroughly understood the position you would be putting me in."

"Jane. You're twisting what happened."

"No, I'm not. You left that vase on my porch on

Sunday while I was at church and you know I always go to church with my mother.''

"All right. I should have—''

"Oh, no. Don't give me any *should haves*. Just tell me. Why did you do that?''

"I wanted you to have the vase. I thought I'd just leave it there, let you find it. A surprise. You left on your own this morning. I thought you'd be coming back the same way. And then I thought there should be flowers. So I went out and I got them. And when I came back, your mother's car was there. I waited till she left. And here I am.''

Now, how had he done that? Made her feel like a complete jerk for doubting his motives? And why had she even brought up her mother? It should not be an issue. There was no reason to quiz a man about his motives unless she *cared* about his motives, unless why he did what he did was important to her.

He stuck his hands in the pockets of his snug black jeans. "Look. I saw that vase in the window of an antique store in Tahoe. I knew it was perfect for you. I knew you would want it. I just…wanted you to have it.''

Oh, this was awful. How had this happened? She felt like an ungrateful, hard-hearted bitch. She swallowed. "Cade. Truly. I can't accept it.''

"Was I wrong?'' His jaw was set, his eyes narrowed to silver slits. "Are you going to tell me that you *don't* want it?''

She backed off a step and crossed her arms beneath her breasts. "What I want isn't the issue here.''

He took a step forward. "Sure, it is.''

"Stop. I mean it. Just stay right there."

He shrugged. "Okay. I'm not moving."

She spoke with great care. "The vase is beautiful. So are the flowers. But I'm sorry. I can't accept them."

His thick, silky lashes drooped down and when he looked at her again, everything was changed. His eyes had gone lazy now—lazy and knowing. "Sure, you can."

"No, I—"

"Jane. It's a gift, and that's all. I don't expect anything in return for it. So there's only one question here. And that is, do you like the damn vase?"

"No, Cade. That's not the question. That's not it at all."

"Yes, it is."

"No."

"Do you like it?"

Neither of them had taken a step since she had ordered him to come no closer to her. So why did she feel as if he'd backed her into a corner?

She went ahead, gave an honest answer. "Yes. I do like the vase. And the daisies. Very much."

Something sparked in his eyes. A gleam of triumph. "You want to keep them."

"Don't put words in my mouth."

"Just admit it. You want them."

He had trapped her again. Either she lied—or she admitted how she coveted his gift. He knew very well what she thought of telling lies. But an admission would only encourage him. "I'm not admitting anything."

"So all right. You want them."

"I didn't say—"

"Damn it. It's a vase. Some flowers. No big deal. Give us both a little pleasure. Take them."

Give us both a little pleasure.

It was an innocent enough remark, in context. Still, the hidden meanings in it caused a hot shiver to slide over her skin. "Listen to me, Cade Bravo." She spoke perhaps more strongly than she should have, her voice going just to the edge of shrillness. "I won't take any gifts from you. I'm not going to go out with you. You just have to accept that. You just have to leave me alone."

Something happened in those silver eyes, a veil going down. There was not even a hint of a smile on those lips now. His face was closed against her. She had that feeling again, the same as in the Highgrade that day when he tried to get her talking and she brushed him off so curtly—that sinking feeling.

That feeling of loss.

He said, very gently, "All right, Jane." And then he turned and went out the screen door.

"Cade!" she called after him. He was halfway down the steps and he didn't so much as pause. "Take your vase and your flowers."

He didn't stop. He didn't turn. He went on down the walk.

"Cade, please."

But he was already gone.

Chapter Six

Jane almost grabbed the vase and chased after him. But what good would that do? He'd only refuse to take it. They'd end up at the same standoff they'd reached just now.

Or worse.

She had to face it. Each time she confronted him, she felt the pull of attraction more powerfully, as if their arguing with each other fed the fire between them. She had to be careful. She could end up going down in flames.

No. She couldn't go rushing after him. She had to settle down a little, get her mind thinking rationally. She stared at the long, narrow table to the right of her open front door, at the bouquet of yellow flowers and the shining golden vase.

All right. Somehow she had to find a way to make

him take back the vase. It didn't matter what he said, about wanting her to have it, no strings attached. Maybe he meant what he said. She would never know for certain. But it simply *felt* dishonest, for her to take his special gift to her and then say no to his advances.

However, she would keep the flowers. They weren't especially expensive and they were perishable. He could hardly return them to the florist for a refund. Keeping them, treating them with care and respect, seemed the graceful thing to do.

Jane took the daisies into the kitchen, filled a big yellow pitcher with water and flower preserver and then arranged the bright flowers, stripping off leaves where necessary, fresh-cutting the stems at a slant. When she was done, she found herself smiling just to look at them, so sunny and cheery. She put them in the center of the kitchen table and then she went back to the front hall and quietly closed her front door.

The next day, when she came home from the bookstore during her lunch break, Cade's low, green car was nowhere in sight. There was no one in the house, at least not that she could see.

She went inside and got the vase and carried it over to his place. Gently she set it by the front door. And then, her face flushed and her silly heart beating way too fast, she ran back to her house. She raced up the steps, yanked back the screen, darted inside and shut and locked the front door behind her.

As if there was some danger. As if locking her door for her lunch hour would keep her safe from him.

When she finished her light meal of fruit and cheese and came out again to return to the store, his car was still gone. And the gold vase still waited on his porch. She hesitated a moment, on the sidewalk in front of his house, worrying that maybe someone else would come by before Cade. That they would see the vase. And take it.

But that was highly unlikely in New Venice, where burglaries were virtually unheard of. No. The vase would be fine where it was. He'd discover it soon enough. There was nothing to worry about.

That night, when she got home, his car was gone. And so was the vase.

Well, good. He must have been home, at least for a little while. Maybe he'd gone on over to Tahoe, to that antique store where he'd found the vase in the first place. He'd sell it back to the dealer. That would be that.

She made herself dinner. After she ate, she took a long, scented bath and then she got into her big old four-poster bed, propped herself up against a pile of pillows and called Celia. Her friend answered the phone on the third ring.

"You busy?"

"Jane. Hello."

Jane heard murmuring. Celia must have put her hand over the receiver. Yes. Celia's soft voice, then Aaron's low rumble.

"You're busy," said Jane.

"No. Not for you. I'm never busy when it's you."

"Hah. Right."

For a long time, before Celia and Aaron became an item, when their relationship was strictly professional, Celia was constantly working. Jane would call and leave messages and Celia would forget to call back.

"I'm a settled, married woman now," Celia said. "I return my calls and take time for my friends."

"But if you and Aaron were—"

"He's always got work to do. You know that. He's already left the room. But don't worry. He'll be back. In a half hour or so—and how are you?"

"Doing all right. How's the baby?"

"Just fine, according to my doctor. But I'm getting fat. Aaron says I'm not. He says I look beautiful. I think I'll keep him."

"A wise decision."

Celia talked about the plans she and Aaron had made. They were going to keep living on-site, at High Sierra, the resort and casino that Aaron ran. They were planning to add a nursery to Aaron's penthouse suite, and Celia was starting to think about hiring a nanny. She loved her job as Aaron's assistant and she planned to go back to work a few weeks after the baby was born.

Celia did sound so happy. There was a lightness, a certain note of joy in her voice now. Jane was glad for her, and yet a little sad, too. A tiny bit envious, though she knew it was small-minded to feel that way. Celia had a husband she adored who loved her passionately in return. And a baby on the way.

Jane put her hand on her own stomach, remembering…

But no. The past was a place it was better not to visit. There were some tender memories there. But such terrible pain, way too much fear…and a gaping hole of loss.

Jane said, "Hey. I heard your husband was handling the bands for the Labor Day picnic this year?"

"That's right. You won't believe who he got." Celia mentioned three different groups. All big stars.

"Wow. I am impressed."

"Has my man got the juice, or what?"

"No doubt about it. And I keep forgetting to ask. Are you two going to be there?"

"Absolutely. We wouldn't miss it. I've already booked us a beautiful room at the New Venice Inn."

"You know you can always stay with me."

Celia sighed. "You know I love to stay with you. But big plans are afoot here."

"Meaning?"

"I'll explain. In a minute—and what about Jilly? Do you know? Is she coming, too?"

"I think so. She didn't give me a definite, but it was close enough."

"*Yes*. That's what I want to hear. It's going to be great. Triple Threat strikes again." Triple Threat was the three of them, Celia and Jillian and Jane. It had been a joke between them, since middle school. They'd called themselves the Triple Threat, when in reality they were three nice, middle-class girls who turned in their homework on time, obeyed their mothers and never cut school.

Jane said, "Now tell me about these big plans."

Celia laughed. "More progress on the Bravo front."

"I'm listening."

"Jonas and Emma will be there."

"At the picnic?"

"That's right. And that's not all. Get this. Marsh Bravo, his wife, their daughter and their baby son are coming, too. I've booked them all at the New Venice Inn, with us. Bravos will be taking over the place for the Labor Day weekend."

"Marsh. That's Cade's half brother, the one who lives in Oklahoma, right?"

There was a silence. Then Celia repeated, "*Cade's* half brother?"

Jane's face felt hot. What a stupid slip. "Well, I meant, *you* know. Aaron *and* Cade *and* Will's half brother."

"Janey, you're backpedaling."

"Oh, well, fine. Whatever. So tell me. What happened with Marsh Bravo?"

"Janey—"

"Come on, tell me. I want to know how this happened."

Celia gave in and let the slip-up pass. "Well, I got Aaron to call him. Marsh lives in Norman, which is near Oklahoma City. His wife is named Victoria, goes by Tory. They were glad to hear from us. Turns out Marsh has no brothers or sisters, except for Aaron, Will and Cade."

"Well, I think that's wonderful. That he called them. That they're coming out here."

"Me, too. I've really wanted this, to see Aaron get to know the other branches of his family at last."

Jane agreed that it was a very good thing. Then Celia asked how the bookstore was doing, how Jillian's latest visit had gone. Jane answered all her questions.

And then, a few minutes later, they were saying goodbye.

Jane picked up the novel she'd been reading, opened it to her place and stared blindly down at the page. She blinked, tried to focus, read a few lines.

But it was no good.

She couldn't concentrate.

She turned off the bedside light and sat in the dark, staring at the open door to the upstairs hall, telling herself she was not going to get out of that bed.

Then she pushed the sheet away and padded to the window.

His lights were on.

He was home.

Her heart did something ridiculous inside her chest.

God. She was hopeless. A totally, completely, utterly hopeless case.

Cade saw the light in her bedroom go out. He wondered if she had as much trouble sleeping as he did lately. He hoped so. He hoped she thought of him. He hoped she suffered like he was suffering. Hoped she was driving herself crazy trying to get him off her mind.

He sat in his completely remodeled den, which was housed in the turret on the side of the house next to hers, and he channel-surfed for an hour or two. There was nothing of any interest on any of the seventy-plus channels available to him. Next to him, on the side table by his reclining chair, sat the gazing ball vase she had left at his door that day. Now and then, he would glance at it, see his own face, bizarre and distorted, all nose and mouth, see the flash and flare as it cast back the images from the TV.

Around eleven, he got up and grabbed his keys and drove over to the Highgrade.

Caitlin was behind the bar. "Something eatin' you, my darlin'? You don't look so good."

"I'm fine, Ma. Give me a draft."

She leaned across the bar at him. He smelled that musky perfume of hers. The top half of her Western shirt had starbursts of purple sequins sewn on it. "Uh-uh. You got a moody look. What's the problem—love or money?"

"Back off, Ma. I only want a beer."

She turned, tapped him a tall one, and set it in front of him. "So what's the good word for the day?"

He drank, then saluted her with the half-full glass. "It's Sunday. I only do the word thing on the week-days."

"So give me Friday's word then."

He drained the glass, set it on the bar. "That would be *loquacious*. Means long-winded. Chatty. Talkative. All the things I'm not tonight."

Caitlin chuckled. "'Nother beer?"

He nodded. She filled his glass again. He carried it into the back room, where he found a game of seven-card stud in progress. He pulled up a chair.

By three in the morning, when the game broke up, he was up a little over a thousand. He drove home, where the rooms were big and empty and the house next-door was dark.

He went straight to the den where the golden vase was waiting.

In the morning, when Jane went out to get the paper, she found the vase back on her porch. He'd put it well to the right of the door, so that she wouldn't damage it by accident when she pushed the screen wide. She didn't see it until she'd picked up the paper from the bottom step, glanced over to see that his car was there, at the curb by his house, and turned back to go inside again.

At the sight of the vase, gleaming silver-gold, back on her porch all over again, her heart kicked crazily against her ribs. Her pulse went racing. Her skin felt hot.

Ridiculous. Absurd.

She slapped her paper against her thigh and went inside, leaving the vase right where it was. She ate her breakfast, read the news over a second cup of coffee and dressed for work.

When she left the house, she left the vase, too, in the exact spot he had put it, on her porch, to the right of the door. At lunchtime, it was still there. She set her mind on ignoring it.

Which, of course, was much easier said than done. The mind, after all, will always find its way to any place you tell it not to go.

That night, at eleven-thirty, she ran out of the energy to keep pretending there was no antique vase on her front porch. She got out of bed and put on her clothes—dark clothes, as a matter of fact, clothes suitable for skulking—and went downstairs.

The vase was still there, right where he'd left it. She looked out at the curb. No sign of his car. Over at his house, the porch light was on, the windows dark.

She knelt and picked up the vase and carried it over there and left it in the same place she'd left it the day before.

The next morning, it was back on her porch.

Jane sighed at the sight of it.

And then she waited, until that night when his car was gone. She took it back over and left it at his house.

The next morning, Wednesday, when she went out to get her newspaper, there it was. She saw it and she smiled.

And right then it occurred to her that it was becoming a game with them—sneaking his gift back and forth between their houses, each so careful to return it when they knew the other wouldn't catch them in the act.

A game. She was playing a game with Cade Bravo.

She utterly disapproved of herself.

And as of right now, she was opting out. She picked up the vase and took it inside and then went out to her garden and clipped an armful of flowers. She arranged them in the fabulous vase, quite artfully, she thought. And then she put the vase in the place of honor in the center of her dining-room table.

A little later, at the store, she made some calls to a few antique dealers in Tahoe. On the fourth call, she hit the jackpot. The dealer remembered the vase.

He'd sold it just the Saturday before, to a gambler flush from some tournament down in L.A.

Yes, she thought. That would be Cade.

She explained that she was considering buying it, asked if he could tell her how much she ought to pay. If he could let her know what he'd sold the vase for, she suggested, that would be terrific.

"Sure," he said, and named a figure.

To double-check, she called more dealers. In Sacramento and in Reno. To each, she described the vase and asked if they were familiar with such a piece. She managed to talk two of them into giving her an educated guess as to the vase's value. Both of those estimates weren't all that far from the amount the dealer in Tahoe had quoted her.

So she made out a check to Cade Bravo.

She chose a nice card from the card rack at the store. It had a picture of the seashore and two children, a boy and a girl, building castles in the sand. Inside she wrote,

Cade,
I've decided to keep the vase. I've called several dealers and I'm reasonably certain I'm giving you a fair price for such a beautiful piece. My check is enclosed.
Sincerely,
Jane

She slipped the check inside the card and put the card in its matching envelope, sealed it, addressed and stamped it. Then she left Madelyn to mind the store for a few minutes and ran across the street to the post office. She felt quite pleased with herself as she dropped the envelope in the mail slot. She had taken a bad situation and turned it around, made it all right.

Things should settle down now, she told herself. She'd solved the problem. She'd paid for what she took from him.

Yes, she felt a little jittery the next couple of days, a little on edge. It was that waiting-for-the-other-shoe-to-drop feeling. Sometimes she wondered what he would do next.

But Thursday passed. And Friday. And nothing happened. By Saturday morning, she was telling herself that the problem was solved. He'd accepted the fact that they couldn't go on playing silly, pointless mind games with each other, sneaking onto each other's porches when the other wasn't looking. Her buying the vase from him was a reasonable solution. He would cash her check and that would be that.

Saturday, his car was again in front of his house and her mail was waiting when she walked home for lunch. She carried it inside with her. Three catalogs, a couple of bills and an envelope addressed to her in a bold, round hand. There was no return address, but the letter had been mailed from in-town, according to the circular U.S. post office stamp.

From Cade.

She knew it without having to open it. She dropped the rest of the mail on the long table by the door and took the letter into the dining room, where she put it down a few inches from the silvery gold vase.

She glared at that envelope, considering. Maybe

she shouldn't even open it. What good could it do her, to find out what was inside? Most likely none at all.

Then again.

It could be something totally innocent, couldn't it? A simple acknowledgment that he'd received the check.

She let out a scoffing sound. Right. Cade Bravo doing something totally innocent.

Not in this lifetime, girlfriend.

She swore, low, a word that her mother would have gasped to hear. And she grabbed the envelope and ripped it open.

There was a card. A card very similar to the one she had sent him. A beach scene. Two children, a boy and a girl. The boy wore shorts and a striped shirt. The girl, a sleeveless white lace dress and a straw hat with a turned-back boat-style brim. They stood very close, the boy holding a conch shell to the girl's ear, their bare toes just touching in the wet sand.

It was lovely. So sweet, their young faces, seen from the side. You could almost hear the boy whispering, ''Listen…''

And the girl had her eyes cast down, lost in the sea sound coming from the shell.

Jane's hand was shaking. She opened the card, found her check waiting there. She moved it out of the way to read what he'd written.

Jane,
What's this? You don't owe me any money.
Hope you are enjoying the vase.
Cade

It was too much. It had to stop.

Clutching the card in her hand, Jane whirled for the front door. She barreled through the screen, letting it slam behind her. When she got to his door, she punched the bell three times in quick succession. When he didn't immediately answer, she fisted her hand and banged on it good and hard.

It opened.

And there he was. Wearing khaki pants, no shoes, and a short-sleeved cotton shirt—unbuttoned.

He had one of those torsos you could scrub your laundry clean on. A real, true honest-to-goodness six-pack of a stomach. Jane stared at it, and blinked, and forced her gaze upward.

Into those silver eyes. "Jane. What a surprise."

"I'd like to come in, please. I don't want to stand here on your front porch and say what I have to say to you."

He stepped back and bowed her over the threshold.

Chapter Seven

He led her to the ground-floor turret room, next to the entry hall, a nearly circular room with windows all around, a room where the furniture, arranged in the center, was big and inviting-looking, mostly camel-colored leather, with a couple of fat easy chairs in an attractive plaid. The tables were mismatched, pleasingly so. The afternoon sun streamed in the tall windows, reflecting warmly off the shining pale wood of the floor.

The room gave her pause. Jane had been in the house once or twice over the years, while the Lipcotts owned it. She'd always thought of it as dark to the point of being oppressive. There had been mahogany paneling, hadn't there? And dark hardwood floors? Cade had opened it up inside, made it friendlier, brighter, more welcoming than before.

Not that it mattered.

She hadn't come here to admire the decor.

He gestured at a big leather sofa. "Have a seat."

She backed up to it—then decided no way she should sit down for this. She stood tall and waved the card at him. "What is this, Cade?"

"Well, Jane. It's a card."

"Oh. Oh, right. A card. It's a *card.*"

"Jane—"

"Don't you speak."

He threw up both hands in an I-give-up gesture. Then he dropped to one of the plaid easy chairs and sprawled there, looking insolent and challenging and maddeningly sexy, with his shirt gaping open around that impossibly hard washboard belly, feral eyes watching her.

She glared down at him. "I am so furious, so livid. So *damn* mad."

"Hey. I can see that."

"Don't you smirk at me."

"Jane—"

"And stop interrupting me. Let me say what I came here to say."

He shrugged, slung one lean leg up on the arm of the chair, rested an elbow on it—and kept his mouth shut.

Now, she could talk. She could tell him off.

Trouble was, all of a sudden, she had no idea where to begin.

He lifted an eyebrow at her, but other than that, he didn't move, didn't make a single sound.

She let out a long, weary breath, thought, *What am*

I doing here, adding fuel to this dangerous fire burning between us?

It was a moment of insight. She saw herself clearly and what she saw wasn't good. She was keeping this thing between them going every bit as much as he was.

Confronting him thrilled her.

And her life, in the years since the disaster of her marriage, had been distinctly short on thrills. She'd told herself she liked it that way. Certainly, at first, she had. But what about now? What about the past few busy, contented—and just a little bit lonely—years?

A deeper, more painful truth dawned. When this silver-eyed charmer finally gave her what she said she wanted—when he left her alone for good—she was going to feel dumped, brokenhearted. Forlorn.

It didn't matter what happened today, or where they went from here. If it ended right now, with whatever they said to each other in this light-filled room, she would miss him. Terribly. Miss the excitement between them, the awareness, the connection of the attraction they shared.

Somehow, without her even realizing it was happening, it had become too late. Too late to tell him off and turn around and walk away and forget him.

When he stopped pursuing her, when he finally lost interest, she would suffer. She would have to go about the painful process of getting over him.

For some reason, her legs didn't feel all that trustworthy. She stepped back and lowered herself to the end of the sofa where she'd refused to sit just moments before. In her right hand, she still held the card he'd sent her. She stared at it, at the two innocent children, the wild surf beyond, and she heard her own voice murmuring, "Oh, I don't...how did this happen? I didn't mean for this to happen...."

She looked up. He was still there, still slouched and waiting, his lean, tanned bare foot hanging over the arm of the chair. He was also still silent, as she'd ordered him to be.

She set the card on the low table between them. Her throat felt tight and dry. She swallowed. "Once I told Rusty to shut up. He hit me."

Oh, God. Had she really said that?

She must have. Something flared in his eyes. His mouth tightened, but he didn't speak.

She sat forward. "Go ahead. Please. Say it."

"I've said it before. I guess you weren't listening. I'm not Rusty."

"No," she said. "You're not. I know you're not. He, um, he hit me a lot."

Cade moved then, swinging his leg to the floor and leaning toward her as she leaned toward him. "I've been in fights. Well, you know that. I've had a chip on my shoulder, I guess you could say. But I never hit a woman, Jane. Never in my whole damn life."

"I believe you. I do." She swallowed again, nodded. "He idolized you, Rusty did. It was always 'Cade Bravo this, Cade Bravo that' with him. I guess I'm holding that against you, a little."

"Jane. I hardly knew him. He was your age, right?"

"Um-hmm."

"Five years younger than me, just another kid with a bad attitude hanging around town. I have to admit, I took a little notice when I heard how he got shot trying to hold up that that Speedy Mart over in Reno, but only to think what a damn fool he was."

"I was the fool. For falling for him, for running off with him, marrying him…" She paused, pressed her lips together in regret and self-disgust. "Just your everyday, classic act of rebellion. Against my mother, against all her rules and restrictions. And against her unhappiness, too, with her sham marriage to my father…well, you know about that, right—I mean, at least about my father and Caitlin?"

He sat back in the chair again. "I heard the rumors. That Caitlin and your father had a thing going years ago."

"I can tell by your voice, by the look on your face, you don't believe there was any affair."

He shook his head. "Caitlin has her standards, hard as that is for some folks to believe. She's been with a married man or two. But never when she *knew* that they were married. As soon as she found out they had wives, they were outta there. She would have known your father was married from the first. So my bet is, she wouldn't have let herself even get started with him."

Jane dragged in a long breath. "I think you're right. That she wouldn't. And she didn't."

He actually looked surprised. "Wait a minute. You know what happened, then?"

"I think so, yes."

"Your mother told you?"

"Hardly. My mother's always…referred to it. Always hated Caitlin, made cruel remarks about her. But she would never talk about what actually happened."

"Your father, then."

"No. My father and I don't talk much. We never have. I wouldn't know how to ask him something like that. I wouldn't know where to begin."

"Then who?"

"My aunt Sophie. I could ask her anything. And I did."

"Ah. And what did Aunt Sophie say?"

"That my dad had a thing for Caitlin. That he went after her and she turned him down. More than once. That she told him to go back to his wife. So he left my mother. Caitlin still wouldn't have him. He came back home and picked up where he left off. My mother accepted his return. But that's about it. They're not close, not in any sense. And my mother won't let go of the idea that it was all Caitlin's fault."

"And she also considers all Bravos guilty by association."

"It's her problem. I know that."

"But?"

"Well, it does make it all the more…difficult, between you and me."

He grunted. She sat back a little, leaned an elbow on the arm of the sofa, looked away and then back at him.

"Go ahead," he said. "You were talking about Rusty."

"It was probably a mistake."

"It's all right. Tell me."

"I think I've said too much already."

"I don't. I think you should go on."

"No. Really. You don't need to hear any more."

That almost-smile came and went on his lips. "Maybe you need to say it."

That made sense. Too much sense. "Yes. All right. Maybe I do."

He nodded. And then he waited.

And soon enough, she was talking again. "I was so crazy for him, for Rusty…" Her voice faded off. She was thinking, *Crazy for him, just like I am for you.*

She blinked, went on. "I thought it was love. What did I know? I was only seventeen when it started. And then, after we got married, I was so sure I could make it work. I *wanted* it to work, desperately wanted to prove myself, as a grown woman, as a wife."

"Yeah, and what did Rusty want?"

A tight sound escaped her. "To get high, to have a good time, *all* the time—with me, while it was new between us…" Again, she wondered, *Should I be saying this? Is this wise?*

He prompted, softly, "But then?"

And wise or not, she told him. "For Rusty, being with me got old. There were other women and there was too much drinking and there were way too many drugs. And the more he got high, the meaner he got. He beat me down. More than my mother ever did. It was physical and it was psychological, too, what he did to me. I went from being crazy in love with him to trying to appease him to being flat-out terrified of him. When he died, I was...broken. It took a long time, before I felt whole again.''

There was a silence. She heard a car going by on the street outside, and the jeering call of a blue jay perched on the fence between their two houses. The jay took flight.

And Cade said, "What else?"

She sat straighter, folded her hands in her lap. "What do you mean?"

"There's something else you almost said. But you held it back."

How had he known? "You know a lot about women, don't you?"

He made a low sound in his throat. "I read faces for a living. I count cards, I remember the order of play—and I watch the other guy, I try to spot his tell. You know what a tell is?"

"A gambler's term, isn't it? The little things a player might do, little gestures and looks, that give his hand away."

"Right. Just now, it was something that happened before you said 'broken.' Your eyes shifted, your mouth got tight. You were going to say more. But you changed your mind."

"I think I've said more than enough." She stood. "Don't you?"

He let his head drop against the back of the chair and looked up at her, a look both lazy and measuring. "How the hell would I know if you've said enough? I don't know what it is you're not telling me."

"It's not important."

"Jane. Shame on you. That was an outright lie."

He was right again. Her cheeks burned. "Yes. It was a lie. What I didn't say *is* important—to me. And I don't *want* to say it. I've said enough." She felt so strange, so raw around the edges, and bewildered, too, like someone suddenly awakened from a sound sleep in a dark room by a bright light glaring full in her face.

She had come storming over here to tell him off— and ended up sitting on his sofa, pouring her heart out.

And now, truly, it was time to go. She told him as much. "I should go now. I have to get back to the store."

He stayed where he was, resting back in that comfortable chair, looking up at her with—what? A sort of friendly intimacy. He asked, "Will you keep the vase? Please. As a gift."

Somehow, it didn't even seem like an issue anymore. "Yes," she said. "I will take the vase. As a gift. Thank you."

He smiled then, a real smile, and he straightened in the chair, gesturing at the coffee table as he rose to his feet. "Take your check."

She picked up the card, slid it in the side pocket of her skirt and then turned for the entrance to the front hall. He followed behind her, to the door.

Before she went out, she couldn't resist turning to him again. "I…"

"Yeah?" He looked hopeful. He didn't *want* her to go.

And really, a few minutes of small talk…how

could that hurt? "I like what you've done. To the house."

"I'm happy with it."

She backed up enough that she could lean against the door. "I heard you had other houses, in Las Vegas and in Tahoe."

"I sold the Vegas house. Lately I'm not there enough to justify the expense." His focus kept shifting—from her hair, to her eyes, to her mouth, as if he couldn't decide which part of her he wanted to look at the most. "And yeah, I have a condo in Tahoe. It's on the market."

She was thinking that she liked it, the way he looked at her, as if he couldn't get enough of looking at her. She liked it a lot.

And wasn't it her turn to talk? "So, you're really settling in here?"

"For now." His gaze had stopped roving. He looked right in her eyes. She stared back—and then couldn't resist looking down a few inches, watching his mouth move as he spoke.

He said, "I'm not a big one for settling in, long-term. I like to keep mobile."

Mobile, she told herself. *He likes to keep mobile. He doesn't want to settle down.*

She got the message. It was pretty hard to miss. He was telling her again, as he'd told her before. Whatever happened between them would not include forever.

She should go.

She stayed right where she was.

He added, "I know folks wondered, that I would buy a house like this."

"Yes, they did wonder." She smiled, leaned more fully back against the door.

"Did you?" he asked.

She was staring at his mouth again. She shook herself. "Did I what?"

He smiled. Slowly. He knew exactly what kind of effect he had on her. Patiently he asked again, "Did you wonder what bad Cade Bravo was doing, buying an old Victorian on Green Street?"

"Not really. After all, *I* have a house on Green Street. And I love it. It's not so hard for me to believe someone else might feel the same."

He moved in closer, rested a hand on the edge of the door, not far from her shoulder. "And your mother—she's pretty outraged, right? 'One of those horrid Bravo boys, living on Green Street!'"

Jane almost laughed. He'd hit Virginia's reaction so precisely.

Cade did laugh, the sound low and sexy and warm. "I nailed her, right?"

"Unfortunately, yes."

He was very close. She could smell him, soap and man and a faint hint of aftershave. "Jane..." And heat. Somehow his body gave off a scent of heat. He whispered, "You gonna let her stop us, let her keep us from each other?"

Dangerous, she thought. She was looking at his mouth. So dangerous. So tempting. So exactly what she longed for. She realized she was biting the inner side of her lower lip. She made herself stop that. "It's not only my mother."

"What else?"

"You know what. We don't want the same things."

"That's right." The very sound of his voice was like a tender hand, stroking. "We want different things. *I* want *you*. *You* want *me*."

"Very funny." She wasn't laughing. She felt kind of hypnotized, her mind slow and thick, but in such a thoroughly lovely way. "That's not what I meant. You know it's not. I meant, in life. We want different things in life."

"So?"

"So it can't...go anywhere. You said that yourself. You're not a man who wants to settle down."

"Is it so necessary, for me to settle down, for a love affair to *go* somewhere?"

"Not as long as you're having that love affair with someone who isn't me."

"But, Jane. I thought you understood. I don't want to have a love affair with someone who isn't you."

"You say that now."

"And I mean it. Now."

"But later—"

"I keep trying to tell you. Forget about later. Later can take care of itself."

"Haven't we been through all this before?"

"Yeah. We're still working on it."

"You mean *you're* still working on *me*."

"Jane, Jane. You have a cynical mind."

"No, I'm realistic. And I have goals. I have hopes

and dreams. I want a good husband. I want babies...."

"There you go with the good, steady man again. The one you keep finding over and over—the one who bores you to death." He tipped his head to the side, as if considering. "Then again, the babies are news. You never mentioned them before."

"I know it's all funny to you. But to me, it's—"

"Shh." He put up a finger, near her lips, but not quite touching them. It seemed, though, that she could feel it—feel that finger, on her skin. "Listen," he said. "I know I'm not what you're looking for, not in the long-term. Not marriage material, not your steady, dependable guy. Not Mr. Right in anyone's book. But I'm here, now. There's this...thing between us. You're single, so am I. It's our damn business what we do behind closed doors."

Her mind seemed to be on hold. Her body was burning. She couldn't help thinking, *He's right. Why not?*

She tried to argue, to call up the principles she made a point to live by. "Cade, it wouldn't be right. Wouldn't be honest."

He swore, a whisper of an oath. He was close enough that his breath stirred her hair. "Tell me you don't feel this—the pull between us."

She let out a small moan. "I can't tell you that."

"Damn right you can't. You'd be lying, if you did. Because it *is* honest, what we feel for each other. Maybe it doesn't come with a lifetime guarantee. But it's palpable. It's real."

"Palpable?" she whispered, surprised that he would choose such a word.

"Yeah. That's right. Palpable. Capable of being touched or felt. My word for Friday."

She was enchanted. "Your…?"

"Every day, Monday through Friday, I learn a new word. You think that's funny?"

"No. No, of course not."

"I didn't go to Stanford, but I'm not stupid, Jane."

"Oh, I know. I know you're not."

He had a dent in his chin—a cleft. All the Bravo boys had it. She imagined herself lifting on tiptoe, pressing her lips there, on the cleft in his chin. He was clean-shaven today, no shadow of beard to make his skin rough. It would be smooth, if she kissed him. Smooth and hot…

He lifted a hand.

It was a crucial moment, a moment of choice. She could slide away.

Or stay, feel his touch.

She didn't move. He laid that hand against her throat. A long shudder took her.

He whispered, "Oh, yeah…"

And then she was lifting her mouth with a starved, low cry.

"Say it," he commanded, his face against her hair. He breathed in, deeply, through his nose, as if he craved the scent of her. "Say what you want."

"A kiss. I want you to kiss me…."

"I'm nuts for you, Jane." He said it in the most lovely, tender, incredulous way.

"Oh, Cade…"

He made a low sound in his throat and pulled back enough that she could see how his eyes crinkled with humor at the corners. "That's it? All I get? *Oh, Cade?*"

"Words seem to have failed me."

"I've left you speechless."

"Well, let me put it this way. If you don't kiss me soon, I think I might explode. It could get very messy. You wouldn't want that."

"Kiss you?"

"That's what I said. Please. Kiss me."

"All right, Jane. I'll do that."

"Now, please."

"Yes, ma'am."

Chapter Eight

His mouth touched hers—so lightly, brushing, back and forth, back and forth.

Jane could hardly believe it: her forbidden dreams of him, coming true at last. Her forbidden dreams only better, because the kiss that never happened in her dreams was happening now. She let out a moan and she slid her hands up, over that hot, hard chest of his, to clasp the back of his neck.

He chuckled against her mouth.

And she yanked him closer with a needful groan.

He didn't object. His wonderful mouth went soft over hers and his body pressed in tight, pinning her against the door.

Jane sighed in delight, kissing him madly, letting her hand glide downward again, along the side of his neck, back to the front of him.

Oh, he was glorious. She traced the shape of him, that deep, strong chest, the wonderful ridges of muscle at the top of his belly, then around, edging under the open side of his shirt, to where the skin stretched taut over the bones of his rib cage. And she didn't stop there. Oh, no. Her fingers danced on, until they caressed the tight curves at the small of his back.

He moaned then, as she scooped at the tender hollow of his spine. And he pressed in even harder, grinding against her, leaving no doubt as to how much he wanted her.

Oh, and she wanted him! So very much. The response of her body to his left her breathless. Arousal moved through her in waves, hollowing her out, leaving that marvelous liquid inner softening. It had been so long, since she'd felt this joyful eagerness, this wonder, this longing. This need...

She moaned again as his tongue found hers. He cupped her face in his hands and he held it, tipped up to him, pressing her harder against the door, drinking the kiss from her mouth.

She was lost in it, in all of it, in the taste and the scent of him, in the feel of him touching her, of *her* touching him. Time stopped. The whole world was right there, captured between them, in the magic of that kiss.

He pulled away in stages, keeping his body pressed to hers, lifting his mouth slightly, then coming back again to kiss her deeply, then retreating, then returning. All the while, he rubbed against her, a sexual friction that drove her wild.

At last, with a low sound that was half regret and

half promise, he opened his eyes and looked down at her. "Jane."

She made a noise, a questioning one. It was all she could manage right at that moment.

"What now, Jane?"

She slumped against the door, drugged with pleasure, longing for more.

"I could carry you upstairs and take all your clothes off and kiss you all over."

She swallowed, licked her lips. "Hmm."

"What does that mean?"

"Hmm. Uh. Well," she said, as if a few garbled sounds constituted some kind of answer.

"Don't tell me. Speechless again."

That was about the size of it. She stared at him for a long time, thinking that this was very nice, just leaning against the door, looking at him, imagining what might happen next.

"What?" he demanded, then shook his head. "All right. I get it."

Since she didn't know what he was talking about, she wisely said nothing.

And he said, "I don't get to seduce you right now."

She thought, *You've already seduced me.* But she didn't say it. It seemed way too dangerous a truth to give him when he hadn't even asked for it.

He added with tender indulgence, "Right now, you have to get back to your store."

Ah. Her store. For a while there, she'd completely forgotten she had a store. "That's true. I do."

"You should see your face. All soft, skin flushed,

mouth swollen. I like it. A lot. I was getting real worried I'd never see you like this.''

She touched his chin—touched that tender Bravo cleft and then his lips, swollen as hers. ''I swore this was never going to happen…''She stroked the side of his face, let her fingers brush the silky hair at his temple. ''But here we are, after all.'' The sad truth intruded. She dropped her hand to her side and added ruefully, ''For a little while, at least.''

He put a finger under her chin, lifting her head to make her look at him. ''Hey. Don't be thinking about it ending. It's barely begun.''

Easy for him to say. She frowned. Slowly the sensual haze was fading, rude reality intruding.

He stepped back. ''What? What is going through your mind?''

She stopped using the door to hold her up, stood straight and brushed at her skirt, not so much because it needed smoothing as for an excuse to look away. ''I'm sorry. It's just that, when I let myself think about it, I get doubtful again.'' She made herself meet his eyes once more. ''I can't help it. There was a time I didn't look ahead, didn't consider what would happen, later, after it was over. I didn't let myself see what a mess it would be.''

''Damn it, Jane. This is now.''

''I know, but a person learns from experience and—''

He cut her off. ''Look. Who knows what will happen this time around? Who the hell can say how it will be?'' The silver eyes narrowed. ''Wait a minute.

You're backing out, aren't you? That's what's happening here.''

"No. I didn't say that.''

"You don't have to say it. It's written all over your face.''

"Hey,'' she said, softly. "What's going on here? Are we arguing again?''

He took another step away. "Yeah. Kind of looks like it, doesn't it?''

There was a long, edgy silence.

Then Cade said, "What do you want to do, Jane? Say what you want.''

"A little time, okay? A little space, to think this over. That's what I want.''

"How long?''

"You would have to ask that.''

"Damn right. I want to know.''

"A couple of days?''

He shook his head. "Great. Tomorrow is Sunday. You can go to church with your mother. She can remind you of what a rotten, hopeless loser I am.''

"You are not a loser. From what I've heard, you do pretty well.''

He grunted. "That's supposed to mollify me, right—and yes, *mollify* was one of my words two or three months ago.''

"Well. Are you mollified?''

"Slightly.''

"Good. And my mother won't remind me of anything—not about you, anyway. I won't be discussing you with her.''

"Well, that's something. I guess.''

She laughed. And then she sighed. "Just a couple of days. Please. I really need them."

"Are you asking me or telling me?"

She wrinkled her nose at him.

"I get it. You're telling. The *please* was just to soften the blow."

"I need to think about this."

"Just admit it. You're telling."

"Okay, I'm telling."

He looked at her, a long look. "Monday night? Can you make up your mind by then?"

Oh, no, she thought. *Monday is way too soon.*

But who was she kidding? She already knew what her answer would be. Really, this was only a last-ditch attempt to put off the inevitable, one last to chance to give herself a serious mental talking-to. She could certainly do that by Monday.

"Monday," he said again. It wasn't a question.

"All right, Cade. Monday."

"Fair enough. I'll come to you. After you get home from the store."

"I'll be there."

Another silence elapsed. There was heat in it, this time, heat and the memory of his mouth on hers, of his hands on her skin, his body pressing in….

She said, "I should go."

"Yeah. Guess so."

She turned and pulled open the door and got out of there.

Jane called Jillian that night but got her answering machine. She hung up without leaving a message.

Then she called Celia. They talked for twenty minutes or so about nothing in particular.

Celia kept asking if Jane had something on her mind.

Jane evaded. Which was doubly reprehensible, in her own eyes. First, because evasion was just next-door to lying. And second, because she'd called her friend with the intention of mentioning what was going on with Cade.

Of asking, *What do you think? What should I do?* Of saying, *I want him so much, but it would only be temporary. An affair. And I know it. And that's not what I'm after.*

And actually, she decided as she went on evading, she had a pretty good idea of what Celia would say, anyway. Celia would come off like a Nike ad.

Go for it. Or was that *Just do it?*

Whatever. Celia would tell her to go where her heart led her. That's what Celia had done, when she fell for Aaron. Aaron had made it very clear to her that he would never marry her.

And look at them now. In the end, Aaron had gone on his knees to Celia—and been happy to be there.

Then again, Celia had known it was love, when she went after him. She really had followed her heart.

If Jane went after Cade, would she be doing that? Following her heart? Hah. Jane had to admit it felt more like something a little lower down.

It felt like lust. A serious case of it. And it was. No doubt about it. Lust was a big part of it.

Was it the only part?

Jane was ashamed to admit that she couldn't be

sure. Couldn't really trust her own battered heart, the heart she had trusted once—and look where that got her. Married to a violent, drug-abusing criminal.

But that wasn't fair. Cade kept telling her he wasn't Rusty. And he wasn't. She knew that.

And hey. There was another bonus with Cade. No chance of her ending up in a bad marriage with him. No chance of a marriage at all.

He'd made that painfully clear.

And she didn't *want* to marry him—did she?

No, of course not. She just plain *wanted* him. As he wanted her.

She said goodbye to Celia and hung up the phone. The night stretched ahead of her, long on indecision and yearning, short on sleep.

Virginia picked her up for church the next morning. As usual, Jane invited her mother in for lunch afterward.

Virginia remarked on the mercury glass vase. "Well, I see you've kept it, whoever gave it to you. Do you know for certain now who that is?"

"Yes, Mom. I do."

"And?"

Jane had her answer ready. "It's a *secret* admirer, Mom," she said lightly. "Which means I can't tell you."

"Oh, that's ridiculous. A ridiculous excuse. I don't approve of this. Of all this mystery."

"Sorry to hear that."

"You're not going to tell me anything, are you?"

"No, I'm not. Iced tea?"

"I don't like this."

"You said that already. Do you want iced tea or not?"

Virginia left at a little after one. Jane went out into the garden and worked until three. The day was just too hot to go on any longer—in the nineties, without even a hint of a breeze.

Sweat was running off her when she gave up and went inside. She was careful, very careful, not to look toward Cade's house. She doubted he would be there anyway. She hadn't seen his car, when she walked Virginia out to the Lincoln.

But she was strictly not looking at his house, not looking for *him*. Until tomorrow. When she would tell him…whatever she would tell him.

And yes, she did know that she was being more than slightly silly, that not looking at his house wouldn't help her with her decision, that it made no difference where she looked, she'd still have to figure out what to do about Cade, what to do about this longing that refused to go away after months of denial, after sleepless night upon sleepless night of telling herself that it would fade.

She went inside and she stripped off her clothes and she stood in the shower—yes, a *cold* shower. When she got out, she was all goose bumps, shivering like mad.

But the longing was still there.

She still wanted Cade.

And that night wasn't any better than the night before.

By Monday morning, she was actually glad she

hadn't told him she had to have longer to make her decision. She was as ready as she'd ever be, she realized that now.

Sometimes, a person had to make like a Nike ad, to behave decisively in spite of the indecision in her heart. She couldn't hang on the edge of her own longing forever. At some point, she had to make the leap.

At noon, she called his house and left a message. "Hi, Cade. It's Jane. Would you call me at the store as soon as you get in?" She rattled off the phone number. "Thanks." And she hung up.

Then she ran to the bathroom and took a shower. She shaved everything that needed shaving. She slathered lotion all over herself and spritzed on scent, reapplied her blusher and mascara and lip gloss. She dressed with care, in her best, most seductive underwear, in a silk chemise-style dress that clung to her curves and would be very, very easy to take off.

She was ready—or as ready as she'd ever be—to become Cade Bravo's lover.

She spent the afternoon jumping every time the phone rang. And every time it rang, it *wasn't* Cade.

By the time she went home, she was certain that *he* was the one who had made a decision. He'd decided he'd be better off not to get involved with her, after all.

On Green Street, the blinds were drawn in his front windows. His car wasn't there. Her feet felt like a pair of lead bricks as she dragged herself up the walk.

Why was this happening to her? All she'd wanted was a nice, steady, average guy.

But no.

She had to go and fall for an impossible Bravo charmer, a guy who'd never held a steady job, who'd run naked down Main Street, who'd made love to more beautiful women than Jane cared to count, who'd come waltzing into her life, bearing a vase with mercury trapped inside it, an armful of yellow daisies—and a relentless determination to break down the walls around her heart.

And all right, all right. It was not specifically her heart he was after. She understood that. And accepted it.

Finally. Now that it was too late.

At seven thirty-five, she was standing at the window in the front parlor, staring out, telling herself she was acting like an idiot. He wasn't coming home tonight, and standing here watching for him to come strolling up her walk wouldn't change what wasn't going to happen.

She was hungry. She should eat.

And yet she just stood there, staring out, watching the street, hearing the cars coming near, watching them pass by, listening as the engine sounds faded away.

At seven forty-two, she heard a car pull up next door. The car stopped. The engine went silent.

She went straight to her entry hall and out her front door. The screen banged shut behind her as she ran down the steps and out into the fading light of the late-summer evening.

He saw her when she was halfway down the walk. He'd emerged from the car. He wore baggy green pants, a white T-shirt, with a short-sleeved shirt un-

buttoned over that. He also wore a look of real pleasure at the sight of her.

He came right for her. They stopped, maybe two
feet from each other, at the end of her front walk.

''I couldn't stand hanging around here waiting,''
he said low. ''I know a place in Tahoe where I can
always pick up a game.''

''I thought you weren't coming.''

He smiled then. ''Ah. Kept you guessin'.''

''You did, you rat.''

There was one of those moments, where they just
stood there and gazed at each other like a couple of
lovesick fools.

Finally he asked, ''Does this mean I get to come
in?''

She reached out and took his hand, reveling in the
shiver of excitement that went through her as he
twined his fingers with hers. ''Come on,'' she said,
and pulled him up the walk.

They barely got in the door before he was kissing
her.

She didn't object. She wrapped her arms around
his neck and she lifted her mouth, sighing with pleasure when his lips met hers.

Chapter Nine

Cade couldn't believe it.

He was in her house. He had his arms around her. Her mouth was open under his, her naughty tongue was playing teasing games. He could feel those incredible breasts of hers, soft and full against his chest. The scent of her, of her smooth white skin and midnight hair, was all around him.

It was happening. At last. Jane was in his arms....

He tangled his fingers in that fabulous hair and fisted his hand, pulling carefully, losing her mouth as her head went back and she gave him her pale neck. He kissed her, in the warm hollow of that smooth throat, his lips on the pulse there, her heartbeat swift against his mouth.

"Nice dress," he said, nuzzling that little hollow between the wings of her collarbone.

She sighed.

The dress had a string around the wide neckline, a string that tied in a bow at the front. He untied the bow. Presto. The neckline loosened in a very accommodating way. He pushed it down, over her shoulders.

"Let me help you," she whispered and she licked his ear.

"Great idea." He stepped back a few inches and watched as she kicked off her low-heeled blue sandals and then pushed the dress free of her arms and down over the fine, full twin question marks of her hips.

The dress dropped to the floor. She looked down at it, then back up at him.

Oh, yeah, he thought. *Oh, absolutely....*

Her bra was navy-blue satin. Her little panties were a match. He drank in the sight of her—all that wonderful hair, those soft brown eyes. Pale skin, with a blush on it. A smile that invited him...

And those breasts. He'd always liked her breasts. There probably wasn't a man who wouldn't. The midnight-blue bra pushed them up so that they looked like they were going to overflow the top of it, spill right out—and into his waiting hands.

She had full hips and rounded thighs and a curving belly. She was not a small woman. She was tall and there was flesh on her, a certain lushness about her. He liked that. A lot. Liked the very naturalness of her that spoke of how comfortable she was, living in her own skin.

So different from the majority of the women he'd known—mostly knock-your-socks-off types who put beaucoups of effort into the way that they looked. To Cade, more and more, over the years, all that effort seemed to smack of desperation.

Jane wasn't like that. Jane was simply Jane. Smart and real and soft, with hair as wild as the side of her he was finally getting to see—and to touch.

On the other hand, he thought, hiding a grin, he *had* seen desperation in Jane. But only to get away from him.

He said, with real enthusiasm. "All this, and we're only a few feet from the front door."

She sighed. "Life is good."

"We're going to need a bed. Very soon."

She looked at him from under her lashes, sending a bolt of pure lust zapping through him. And she murmured, "There's something else we need. I suppose I should have thought of it...."

She was right. "Condoms."

She nodded.

He had plenty. Over at his place.

If he went to get them...

Damn. He could see it all now. He'd come racing back over here with a handful of little foil-wrapped packets, only to find her fully dressed, a scowl on her face and "I've changed my mind" on her lips.

"Jane?"

"Hmm?"

"I've gotta ask."

"Anything."

He liked the way she said that. "If I leave for three minutes, will you promise not to change your mind about this?"

"I promise," she whispered. "I'm not going any-where."

"Good." He pulled the door open, then couldn't resist turning back for one last look. Incredible. She slayed him. She'd damn well *better* be there when he got back. "Stay right there. Don't go anywhere."

"Where would I go? I'm almost naked."

"Stay that way."

"Oh, I will," she whispered. "I promise, I will."

He took off at a run, the screen slamming behind him, down her walk, up his, onto his front porch. He stuck the key in the lock and let himself in—remem-bering just in time to disarm the alarm. Then he was taking the stairs two at a time, racing into the master suite, grabbing what they needed.

He was down the stairs, out the door and running up her walk again in what felt like ten seconds flat.

The inner door was open a crack. He yanked back the screen and shoved the door inward and—

She wasn't there.

He knew a stark second or two of hot fury born of his long-term state of frustrated lust. He wanted to break something, to snap something in two. He saw himself throwing his head back, screaming her name.

But then he got it—she'd left him a trail: her dress over there and a sandal beyond that. That midnight-blue bra draped over the landing halfway up, back strap trailing onto the stair right below.

He let out the breath he hadn't realized he was holding. And he shut and locked the door.

Then he followed where her clothes led him, pick-ing up each item as he got to it, starting with the dress, which was soft and silky and—he couldn't resist pausing to bury his nose in it—scented of her. He reached the first sandal, scooped it up. And he mounted the stairs, stopping on the landing to pick up the bra, hooking an index finger under one of the shoulder straps, lifting it—still warm from her body— twirling it on the end of his finger. Because she had left it there. Because he could.

Directly ahead of him, on the wall of the landing, was a framed portrait of a high school-age girl with Jane's hair and eyes, but dressed in the tight-waisted, full-skirted style popular way back in the 1950s. Cade knew who she was. Jane's aunt Sophie. She used to drive one of those old narrow, high Volkswagen buses and she taught English at New Venice High. Everybody knew you didn't mess with Miss Elliott. She was tough and smart and funny, too. Always one step ahead of a troublemaker like Cade.

He went on, up the second half of the stairs. The other sandal was waiting for him at the top. He bent and grabbed it.

Then he saw the blue satin panties, in front of the first door opposite the stairs, to his left. He moved to them swiftly, scooping them up and laying them over his arm with the dress and the bra.

The door to the room in front of him was open.

It was a large bedroom, with walls papered in roses on a blue ground, walls trimmed out in cherrywood— the window frames, the plate rails, the fireplace, too, which was on the wall opposite the doorway where he stood. A pair of comfortable-looking easy chairs faced the fireplace and there were a number of shut cherrywood doors—to closets and the bathroom, more than likely.

The bed, a big old four-poster, piled high with pillows and covered with a pale crocheted spread, stood on his right, footboard out, headboard against the wall. It had matching nightstands, little tables with lamps on them, one to each side. On the far side of the bed, the wall opened up into the turret, which was smaller than the one at his place, but otherwise much the same, a pentagon of windows looking out on her yard and his yard and Green Street beyond.

Jane stood there, in the turret. Naked.

She was staring out the central window, through the white lace curtains that covered the glass. Outside, the day was fading, but not yet completely gone. The sun had dropped well below the rim of the mountains. Behind her, to her left, on the turret wall nearest the fireplace, a compact spiral stair led up to another room above.

She was a study in shadow. He took a good, long look—because he could. Because she didn't turn or say a word or signal him in any way that she even knew he was in the room with her.

He liked everything he saw. From the dark mass of her hair, to the smooth shape of her shoulders, the incurving waist, the rising swell of her hips. It was all good—all of her, all the way down to her pale bare feet.

Good and...somehow not quite real. It almost felt like this was all some magical, impossible dream he was having.

He ached to get his hands on her, to prove to himself that this really was happening. At the same time, he could have stood there, just looking, forever.

She still hadn't turned toward him.

He looked down at himself. Definitely overdressed.

He went and set her clothes on one of those easy chairs by the fireplace, placing the sandals side by side on the rug. He took off his own shoes and socks, tucking the socks inside the shoes, placing the shoes next to her sandals. He removed his shirt, pulled the T-shirt over his head and laid both on the chair arm opposite her dress.

She still hadn't turned, had given zero indication she knew he was there, in her room with her. But by then, he was certain she knew damn well. He smiled to himself, and took the handful of condoms out of the pocket he'd stuffed them into a few minutes before. He set the condoms on the chair cushion long enough to remove his pants and his boxers and toss them on the chair arm with his shirt.

Then he grabbed up the foil pouches and approached her, stopping no more than a foot behind her.

"Jane."

She didn't answer, not in words. But she did turn her head to the right, her chin down, a move that acknowledged him, accepted him—and invited him, too.

He transferred the contraceptives to his left hand. Then he smoothed the veil of her hair aside, so he could see the tender smile on her lips, the way her dark lashes lay like fans against her cheeks.

She looked back out on Green Street again. "I've

stood here, in this exact spot, a lot in the past few months.'' She spoke softly, to herself, it seemed, as much as to him. "I've stood here with all the lights off, looking at your house, telling myself to stop acting like an idiot. But then not stopping. Staying right here. Looking for signs that you're at home—for the glow of a lamp in a room, for just a glimpse of you through a window…''

"I've done that myself, looking for you.''

"I know you have.''

They were silent. It was a good kind of quiet—surprisingly comfortable. And yet exciting, too. He felt the promise in it, the anticipation.

And from her, he sensed willingness. The willingness to have him, here, with her now. It soothed something down inside him, made a calmness beneath the urgency—after all the bleak months of wanting and waiting—to lay his claim on her at last.

He stepped in even closer, lifting his hand to touch her again, running the backs of his fingers down the side of her throat, out along the warm, silky skin of her shoulder, down her arm. He felt a shiver move through her as his knuckles skimmed her flesh. That shiver pleased him.

He touched her wrist, sliding his hand on down to cradle hers, the back of her hand nestling against his palm. She readily opened her fingers enough that he could slip his between them.

He moved in closer still, wrapping his other arm around her. "You think this'll be enough?" He opened his hand.

She looked down at the condoms. "What? Only seven?"

He chuckled. "I can always get more."

"Well, okay then. We'll manage."

He closed his fist around the condoms as she touched the gold bracelet that gleamed on his wrist and he whispered, "World Series of Poker, No Limit Hold'em. Two years ago."

"That's the big one, right?"

"Yeah. At Binion's, downtown Vegas. Winner takes the gold bracelet—and over a million in prize money. The money goes…wherever money goes. But no winner will ever let go of the bracelet."

"I remember when you won." She was smiling. He could hear it in her voice. "Made the front page of the *Record*."

"Yeah. Big news in New Venice, local loser makes good…"

"I read that article. Nowhere in it were you called a loser. And it *is* a big thing. You should be proud."

He brushed a kiss against her neck. "Yes, ma'am."

"I am serious."

"So am I."

"Serious in yes-ma'aming me, or seriously proud?"

"Both."

"Hmm. All right. I can live with that answer."

"Glad to hear it." Her bare shoulder looked especially inviting right then. He kissed it.

Sighing, she let herself lean back, all those shadowed curves and hollows, soft and warm and smelling so good, settling close, resting against him. He released her hand and brought that arm around her, too, pulling her closer still, feeling her quick indrawn breath as his arousal tucked itself against the small of her back.

"Remember," she whispered after a moment, "that time you asked me to dance? At that party for Celia and Aaron, the one put on by his company, in Las Vegas?"

He remembered all right. He accused, gruffly, "You made me crazy."

"Well, I knew that wasn't any gun you had in your pocket."

He nuzzled her hair. "You're such a comedian."

"You were trying so hard not to hold me too close."

"Hard," he said. "That would be the word for it." He cupped one of those heavy breasts. She groaned. He liked the sound of that. A lot. Her nipples were dark, puckered with excitement. He ran his thumb over one and she gasped.

And that did it. He couldn't resist sliding his hand down, over the curve of her belly, into the dark, thick curls between her white thighs.

She stiffened, gasped again.

"Jane," he whispered, brushing his lips against the side of her face, into her hair, along her cheekbone, at the hollow of her temple. "Jane, Jane, Jane…"

The stiffness left her. She went easy in his arms, parting her legs a little, giving him access. He insinuated one finger between the protective folds of tender flesh. She dragged in a ragged breath, moaned a little, leaned more fully back against him, lifting the mound of her sex a little, offering it to him.

"Yeah," he whispered against the wild tangle of her hair. "Oh, yeah…"

For a while, he teased her, running his finger up over her belly, and down, caressing the side of her waist, the flare of her hip, sliding his palm along the outside of her thigh. He petted her, rubbed the heel of his hand against her, but he held back from parting her, from delving in.

For a while….

And then, when he did touch what she was offering him, he found her as he wanted her. Wet and ready. He dipped a finger in, and then another. She was moving by that time, her hips rocking, making little moaning sounds, her head rolling back and forth against his chest, her hair electric, crackling, clinging to his skin.

He wanted…more. All of her. To touch her. To hold her. To *know* her. All over.

The condoms in his left hand hindered him. He let them go. They spilled to the rug at their feet. She laughed, low in her throat—and then she cried out as he touched her more deeply than before.

He turned her, guiding her around to him, and he moved his hand forcefully in her. He looked in her eyes. They were wide, dazed, far away. And yet also right there, with him, with what he was doing to her, with the sensations he roused in her.

She whispered his name, low.

"Yeah," he said, stroking her deeply, in rhythm with her rising need. "Say it again. Say my name…"

Her eyelids quivered shut.

"No. Come on, Jane. Look at me. Say my name…."

She made a frantic, wild sound. And her lids fluttered open, her brown eyes met his.

"Yeah," he said, then asked gently, encouragingly, "Yeah?"

And she gave him what he wanted. "Cade," she whispered, the sound hot and husky. "Oh, Cade…"

And then she cried out again. Her body bucked wildly. He felt the contractions around his fingers, her climax rolling through her. He held her, going with it, following her body's cues with his hand.

Her knees buckled at the end. She moaned, dragging at him, wanting to go down. He had no problem with that. He went down with her, onto the rug, among the scattered condoms.

Her pleasure quivered on the crest, then slowly faded to afterglow.

They rested, stretched out there, together, on the rug in the turret, with the spiral staircase turning toward the ceiling above them and the summer night falling beyond the windows. He kept his hand on her, in her, feeling that softening, so that her inner body itself seemed to have melted, gone completely liquid. He knew that going into her would be the sweetest thing, the warmest, most welcoming thing.

And he also knew he couldn't wait too long, let the afterglow fade down too far, let her body begin to close itself against him. He wanted her that way, in that perfect state of readiness, the first time he entered her.

With some regret, he pulled his hand from her. She sighed, softly, looking at him in the dazed and open way of a woman satisfied, a woman ready for whatever would come next. He couldn't resist licking his own fingers, tasting her, scenting her, there, on his hand.

She watched him do that, her pupils widening, lips going lax, infinitely soft. He reached out, slid his hand, still wet from her and from his own mouth, into her hair, cupping the back of her head, bringing her to him.

He kissed her. It was all one—his mouth, her mouth. And the taste of her, passing between them, from his tongue to hers.

Still kissing her, he reached over her and picked up one of the condoms. To deal with it, he had to surrender her mouth.

She watched him as he slid it on, looking so open and soft and easy, on her side now, where he'd pulled her when he kissed her, raised up on an elbow, that glorious hair tumbling down her shoulder, veiling her arm and one ripe, full breast.

Was this real? He wondered again, at the two of them, here at last, doing all the things he'd known, deep inside himself, were never going to happen.

She was his now—or she would be, very soon.

His.

He realized what he felt for her was something different. Something new to him.

It was a need to claim, to make something private, between them. Something they shared only with each other.

He wondered what was really going on here, inside his head…and his heart.

Strange. To find himself thinking about his *heart*.

He'd always believed himself immune to the urges that a lot of other men felt. Never had he wanted to make a bond with a woman, to make something between them that would last beyond the moment, beyond the wanting and the taking, beyond the sweet mutual gift of sexual release.

But with Jane…

No. He pushed the dangerous, half-formed thought away. Now was not the time for it. He would think about it later.

Right now, there was Jane. *All* of Jane. To be tasted and enjoyed.

She reached out a hand. And she touched him, curving her fingers around him, at the base. He groaned—and he was damned lucky he didn't lose it right there.

And then she was rising up, sliding one of those slender white feet across his belly, gliding on top of him, capturing him between her smooth, full thighs. She rose higher, up on her knees, one leg on either side of his hips.

He looked at her above him, at the wild tangle of her hair, at her soft, flushed face as she stared down at him through lazy, slitted eyes. He didn't dare look any lower. He groaned, let his head drop back.

And she lowered herself onto him.

Paradise.

No other word for it. Paradise on earth, to be inside

of Jane, her wet heat surrounding him, those fine thighs gripping him...

She moved.

He knew he would die.

"Wait." He made a ridiculous, garbled sound as he grabbed for her, pulling her down tight onto him, holding her there. "I can't..."

She moaned. He opened his eyes in time to see her raise her arms and lift her hair, tossing it, inky and wild in the gathering darkness. He watched her head fall back, her white neck stretching.

"Oh, you can..." She lowered her head again, her eyes meeting his, moving, rocking on him, though he tried to hold her still. "Cade. You know you can..."

"Jane..."

"Oh, yes. Oh yes, you can..."

"Wait. Jane."

"Come on, you can. You know you can."

He made more pleading sounds. And then he couldn't help it. He wanted her moving every bit as much as he needed her still.

He stopped restraining her, let her have him, let her do what she wanted, move as she willed. He dared to look up at her, at all of her, as she rose and came back to him, sliding away and then claiming him fully, her heat and wetness drawing on him one second, then almost lost to him the next.

He let his hands slide upward over her rib cage, his thumbs under her breasts, pleasured by the fullness of them, the womanly weight. He claimed them, cupping one in either hand, loving the size and softness of them, the way the hard nipples pressed into his palms.

He moved with her, wildly, and then slowly, and then faster again. He felt his climax coming long before it took him, rolling toward him, like a huge, wild, obliterating wave.

The wave broke, at last, and he took her hips again, hard, stilling her, pressing himself up into her as he came. She fell then, her upper body dropping against him, her inner muscles contracting as she whimpered in his ear, finishing right with him, going over the moon, beyond the rainbow, past the most distant star in the summer sky.

He wrapped his arms around her and held her tight. He wasn't letting go of her. She had too much that he wanted.

She thrilled him.

And at the same time, she felt like something he hadn't even known he'd been looking for, like the answer to the question he'd been asking himself for over a year now, to what had started with his buying the house next-door and nagged at him all the harder as he found himself noticing her, realized he was attracted to her—hell. More than attracted to her.

That he hungered to get his hands on her.

That he wanted her, bad, in a bed. Or on a floor. It didn't really matter where. Anyplace. As long as she was naked against him.

And that was it, or so he'd thought.

An itch that needed scratching. More powerful, maybe, than the itches that had gone before. But workable. Something that would leave him in peace eventually—and maybe even sooner if he could just get his hands on her, put an end to the mystery. Prove to himself that she was only a woman like any other woman.

But now, well, his attitude had changed.

Everything was different.

Because she was so much more than that, more than her beautiful lush white body, more than an itch he yearned to scratch.

What was it, this thing he felt with her, when they talked, when they laughed together, when he held her—and when he didn't?

Maybe it was crazy, maybe it was next-door to nuts, edging up to downright impossible.

But being with Jane Elliott felt to him like coming home.

Chapter Ten

For a long, lovely time, Jane lay there, using Cade for a mattress, lying limp against his hard chest. She listened to his heartbeat, smiling dreamily to herself, feeling utterly satisfied.

But eventually, a muscle in her calf started twitching. And she noticed that the old wool rug was digging into her knees. She tried to slide to the side.

Cade made a noise of protest deep in his throat, "Uh-uh," and held on.

She kissed him, right next to his ear. "I can't lie on top of you, squashing you, forever."

"Why not?" he growled. The question must have been rhetorical, because as soon as he asked it, he let her go.

She stretched out on her back beside him and felt for his hand. He gave it, bringing hers to his lips, kissing the back of it, then settling their joined hands on the rug between them.

Again, there was stillness. It surprised her, how comfortable she felt with him, how natural and unforced. Really, she'd never felt that way with anyone—well, except maybe Ceil and Jillian. And with them, it was about friendship, which was a whole other thing than this.

Finally she turned her head to smile at him. "Hungry?"

"A little. You?"

Her stomach chose that moment to growl. "A lot."

Cade wanted a shower, so Jane showed him which door led to the master bathroom. He disappeared beyond it. It was fully dark by then. She got up and switched on a lamp and gathered up the scattered condoms, leaving them on the little table to the right of the bed.

Then she joined Cade in the shower. There were kisses. And caresses. Jane thought it a very satisfying way to get clean.

After that, Cade put on his pants and Jane pulled on a robe and they went downstairs to make sandwiches and pour themselves a couple of big glasses of milk. They carried the food back up to her bedroom and got up on the bed where they sat, crosslegged, facing each other, munching away.

Cade said, "That's your aunt Sophie, that picture on the stairs, right?"

Jane chewed and swallowed and grinned at him. "My grandfather Elliott had that painted, the year she graduated from high school. She was something, Aunt Sophie. Did what she wanted and lived her own independent life. And she always...supported me.'' She gestured widely, indicating all that surrounded them. ''I mean literally, of course. This was her house and her money made it possible for me to open my bookstore. And more than that, she always made me feel that she was totally on my side. Even during the worst of times, even when I ran off and married Rusty, Aunt Sophie never turned her back on me.''

He tipped his head to the side, studying her. ''But other people did turn their backs on you, right?''

She bit her lip, shrugged.

He knew. ''Your mother?''

She nodded.

''That's cold.''

Since Caitlin Bravo's stormy relationship with her sons had always been a subject for the New Venice gossip mill, Jane couldn't resist asking, ''Are you trying to tell me that Caitlin never got fed up with you?''

''No. If I told you that, it would be a lie. And if I'm going to hang around you, I've got to stick with the truth. Right?''

She wasn't sure she trusted that gleam in his eye. She said, carefully, ''The truth would be much appreciated.''

''Don't hedge. The truth is expected—isn't it?''

''Yes.'' She frowned. ''But why does that sound like a trick question?''

''A trick question? From me?''

She laughed. ''That's what I said. And about Caitlin...''

"All right. Yeah, sure. She got fed up with me. She would yell and throw things and call me—and my brothers—some pretty ugly names. And then, with her, there was also the problem of her just *being* her. That meant all the men. And the way we lived, over the bar. Yeah, okay. We might have done some pretty crazy things, the three of us—me especially. And I guess a lot of it was just par for the course, natural that we'd be wild, considering the kind of life we lived with her. But still…"

"What?"

"Well, deep down, we always knew she'd kill for us if she had to. She'd die for us without so much as batting those false eyelashes of hers. Never, no matter what stupid, crazy stunt we pulled, would she ever have turned her back on us."

Jane found she could almost envy him—to grow up knowing that kind of passionate devotion from a parent. So strange. She'd always felt a little sorry for those bad Bravo boys. They weren't outcasts in town, exactly. But they came pretty close. And now, listening to Cade, she realized that those boys had had something in Caitlin that pampered, well-behaved, well-brought-up and well-to-do Jane Elliott had never known. They'd had a parent who loved them unconditionally.

Jane did want to be fair, though, to her own parents. "My mother and father didn't cut me out forever. They got over it, eventually—over my running off with Rusty. We reconciled."

He had that watchful look. "When was that?"

She sat back a little. She didn't like this—his sudden watchfulness, or the sharp turn the conversation had taken, edging way too close to territory she had no desire to enter.

She said, carefully, "My parents and I reconciled before Rusty died."

"When you lost the baby?"

She stiffened—and then she told herself to relax. It wasn't all that surprising, that he would know about her miscarriage. She'd been in the hospital. Word had gotten around.

He said, as if in answer to the question she hadn't even asked, "I think I heard about it—about the baby—when I heard about Rusty getting himself killed."

"You heard what?"

"That Rusty was dead. And that it had to be all the rougher on you, since you'd just lost a baby a few months before."

"Well." She swallowed. "Yes. That's right. That's what happened."

He seemed to be waiting for her to tell him all of it.

But she didn't want to tell him all of it. She didn't want to go into it. The horror of her marriage to Rusty Jenkins was behind her now. She wanted to leave it that way.

Cade said, "That was it, right? It was about the baby, the other day, at my house. When you said you were *broken,* but didn't say exactly why?"

She pressed her lips together, nodded. "Yes. That was it."

"So..." He let the word trail off, clearly waiting for her to say more.

She asked, too sharply, "What?" She was thinking about honesty, about the whole truth that she simply didn't want to share.

"You made up with your parents." His tone was gentle. "They stood by you in the end."

"Yes, they did."

"But they hurt you, too, a lot, when they cut you off for marrying the wrong guy."

"That's true. But I hurt them first. I knew they wouldn't approve of Rusty, so I made sure they never knew about him. Then, out of nowhere, as far as they were concerned, I ran away and married him. They felt betrayed. Tricked. And really, I did betray them. I tricked them every time I snuck out to meet him, every time I invited him over when I knew they wouldn't be home."

He said nothing, only looked at her. A probing kind of look. Then he turned and picked up his milk from the bedside table. He drank from it and set it back down. She wondered what he was thinking.

He didn't make her wonder long. "I gotta ask. Is that what'll happen with us?"

"What do you mean?" she said, as if she didn't know.

He gave her a look that said he knew that *she* knew exactly what he'd meant. Then he went ahead and clarified, "Am I going to be another big secret you keep from them?"

It was a yes or no question—and she answered with

evasion. "This is a completely different situation. I'm a grown woman now."

"What does that mean, Jane? Will you tell them about us, or not?"

She turned and picked up her own milk from the night table behind her. When she faced him again, he was waiting with one eyebrow raised.

She blew out a breath. "You said it yourself, the other day, when you were trying to talk me into doing what we just did a little while ago. That you're single and so am I and it's our business what we do behind closed doors."

Her answer hadn't pleased him. His mouth was tight. "Behind closed doors. So that's what we're up to here. No one's gonna know, right? We'll be sneaking between our houses, getting in a quickie when we're both sure no one else will be dropping by. When we get invited to the same places because of Aaron and Celia, we'll act like we hardly know each other. We'll smile and say hi and then turn and walk away."

She took a sip of milk and then set her glass back down. Carefully. "Cade. I didn't say that."

Something flashed in those silver eyes, something dangerous. "Then let's go out. To Bennett's Steak House. You and me. Tomorrow night." Bennett's was arguably New Venice's best restaurant. It was on Main, across and down from Jane's bookstore and the Highgrade.

Stalling and not liking herself very much for it, Jane picked up the second half of her sandwich. She stared down at it, thinking that if Cade took her to

Bennett's, it would be all over town within a day or two. Everyone would know that something was going on between Jane Elliott and wild Cade Bravo. Did she want the whole town to know? It wasn't going to be pleasant, when the story got back to her mother....

"Forget it, Jane."

She blinked and looked up at him. "I didn't—"

"You hesitated. Way too long. You know you did. So just forget it." He turned and set his empty plate on the nightstand behind him.

"Cade. Please..."

The look on his face said it all. She had hurt him. And he wanted the subject dropped. Now.

Jane sat up very straight. "Cade, I'd love to go to Bennett's with you tomorrow night."

"Yeah, right."

"I would. I *will*."

"Jane?"

She sat forward, eagerly, hoping he'd give in and give her another chance on this issue. "Yes?"

He looked...sad. And a little bit tired. "Let it go."

"But—"

"I mean it." His voice was soft. His eyes weren't. "Let it go."

What could she say? "Yes. Yes, all right." She'd blown it and she knew that she had. Her appetite had vanished. She dropped her sandwich on the plate and put the plate on the nightstand behind her.

When she faced him again, he was still looking at her.

She made herself meet those eyes of his, feeling awful, wishing she could turn back the clock, have him ask her out all over again. This time, she wouldn't mess up. She'd answer yes straight out, no hemming and hawing and putting him off.

Oh, what was the matter with her? In recent years, she'd prided herself on how much she'd changed and grown since the disaster of marrying Rusty.

But now she couldn't help wondering, where was the change? Where was the growth? Here she was, making love with a man again at last. Loving every glorious, erotic minute of it. And then stalling at the idea of being seen in public with him, worrying about what her family might say.

"Jane." He touched her bare knee, gently, reassuringly. "It's okay."

"No, it's not. But you're kind to say so."

He took the facing of her robe, which had fallen away, and smoothed it over her knee, tenderly, protectively. Then he caught one end of the sash she'd tied around her waist and gave it a tug. Her robe fell open.

"Hey," she cried, her mood lightening when she saw the gleam in his eye. "What's going on here?"

"Nobody calls me *kind* and gets away with it."

"Oh. Well. I'm so sorry."

"Prove it."

Oh, I will, she thought, as she scooted backward, giggling. She'd blown it once. She wouldn't blow it again. The next time he asked her out, she'd give him an unequivocal yes—in fact, she'd *do* the asking, if he took too long to try again.

He leaned forward, moving to his knees. And she

leaned back, uncrossing her legs. He settled between them. It felt really good to have him there.

"About your aunt Sophie." He was resting on his forearms, kissing her eyelids, her eyebrows, the bridge of her nose…

"Mmm?" She wrapped her arms around him—and her legs, too.

"I really did like her."

"You did?" She ran both hands down the glorious musculature of his bare back. He was still wearing his pants. They'd have to do something about that soon.

He nibbled her earlobe. "Yeah. Had her for bone-head English, in tenth grade. She called me charming and incorrigible."

"Aunt Sophie was no fool." She groaned as he slid down her body—just low enough to latch onto her breast. He drew on the nipple. She groaned some more.

He lifted his head and winked at her. "I had to look up incorrigible. And it wasn't easy, let me tell you. At first, I thought she had said 'encourage-able.' But I could tell by her tone that couldn't be right. I knew it was some other word—but I had no idea how the damn word was spelled."

"That was Aunt Sophie," she whispered breathlessly. "Always finding clever ways to motivate her students." He lowered his head to her breast again. She cried out. "Oh! Oh, yes…"

And then he was moving again…lower.

And lower…

Jane gave herself up to the incredible things Cade Bravo knew how to do with his mouth and his hands.

* * *

Cade opened his eyes. It was still dark. He stared up at the ceiling. Not his ceiling. Jane's.

He was at Jane's. With Jane. In Jane's bed.

He rolled his head and looked at her. She looked good. Soft and sweet, her dark hair all tangled and wild on the pillow. Sound asleep.

The digital clock on her side of the bed glowed at him through the darkness: 3:10 a.m.

Time to get out. Now. While she was still sleeping.

Carefully he turned on his side, facing the edge of the bed, away from the woman sleeping so peacefully beside him. In one slow, even movement, he slid out from under the blanket and lowered his feet to the floor.

Chapter Eleven

Jane woke to morning light. Memories of the night just past came flooding in. She blushed. Her body felt...well used. Well-satisfied. A little bit tender in certain places, but in a very nice way.

She was smiling when she turned her head toward *his* side of the bed.

Empty. She sat up. "Cade?"

No answer. She tossed back the covers and checked the bathroom.

Not there.

Without a stitch on, she ran down the stairs, checked the family room and the kitchen and the parlor and the central hall. In the dining room, the gorgeous vase he had given her gleamed on the table.

But no Cade.

She ran back upstairs and pulled on some shorts

and a shirt, then raced down again, flying straight for the door, flipping the latch, hauling it open, banging through the screen.

His car was gone.

She sank to the porch steps, hung her head and stared down at her bare feet.

Well, all right. He had left. He had a right to leave. It wasn't exactly considerate behavior, but it was certainly nothing for her to get crazed over. She had no claim on him.

Just the opposite. She'd as good as turned him down when he asked her to dinner. And she'd made it pretty darn obvious she hoped her mother and father would never know what was going on between them. She had probably hurt him. And she had no right to expect him to be here this morning.

But wait a minute.

Jane flipped her sleep-snarled hair back off her face and sat up straight. He did have a garage, on the far side of his house, in back. Maybe for once, he'd decided to use it. Maybe he'd gotten up and gone somewhere and come back and parked in the garage and...

Jane let her head hang down again and rediscovered the view of her feet. "Oh, give it up, you fool," she muttered aloud. He was gone. Out of here. Not at home.

Still....

Well, she might as well check—just in case. She got up and padded down her walk and up the driveway south of his house. There was a window on the north-facing wall of the detached garage. She peeked in it.

No Porsche.

So all right.

He really had left.

"Deal with it," she said out of the side of her mouth. "And for heaven's sake, stop talking to yourself."

She trudged back down the driveway and up the walk to her house. When she got to the door, she went in without letting the screen bang shut behind her.

It wasn't too bad. At first.

She got the coffee brewing and she took a shower and she ate her breakfast and walked to her store.

As her lunch break approached, she was aware of a rising feeling—of hope, of anticipation. She walked home fast, feeling breathless and giddy—until she turned the corner onto Green Street and saw that the Porsche still wasn't there. She dragged herself the rest of the way home.

Caitlin, behind the wheel of the shiny black Trans Am she'd owned for at least a quarter of a century, drove up just as Jane was slogging up her front walk. The black car slid to a stop at the curb in front of Cade's house.

Jane lingered on her walk, watching as Caitlin got out of the car. The bright midday sun caught the sequins on her shirt so that they glittered boldly. The ends of the bright bandanna she always tied around her neck waved jauntily in the breeze.

"Hey," Caitlin called. "How you doin', Jane?"

"All right. You're here to pick up Cade's mail?"

"Yeah, sweetie." Caitlin came around the front of the low black car and started up Cade's front walk.

Jane just had to ask. "Uh, Caitlin?"

Caitlin stopped. Turned. "Yeah, darlin'?"

"Well, I was just wondering. Um, is Cade gone then, for a while?"

"Who knows? I'm his ma—and that's about all. He calls and asks me to keep an eye on things when he goes. And then he calls when he gets back. I don't get the details, like where the hell he is or how long he plans to be gone."

"Oh. Well, of course. I understand."

Caitlin was frowning, her head tipped to the side. "You all right, hon?"

Jane smiled instead of answering. "You have a good day, now."

"You know," Caitlin reminded her, "you promised you'd come in the Highgrade and see me sometime."

"I did. And I'll get over there. For lunch. Real soon."

"Don't let me down."

"I won't. Sincerely."

Caitlin waved and went on up the walk. Jane did the same, telling herself that she could stop getting her hopes up every time she came home. If Cade had asked Caitlin to watch his house, chances were he'd be gone for several days.

Her hopes were stubborn, though. That evening, her silly heart beat faster as time to close up approached. She pretty much ran all the way to Green Street.

When she saw that he wasn't home, she trudged the rest of the way to her front door.

She called his house. He didn't answer, of course, since he wasn't there. She left a brief message, asking him to please call her back as soon as he got the chance.

Then she called Celia. They talked for an hour. It was the same as the last time she'd called her friend. Celia kept asking if she had something on her mind. And Jane kept evading. Somehow, she just couldn't bring herself to talk about Cade. Though she wanted nothing so much as to unburden her aching heart, somehow, she could not get the words out.

She kept herself from calling Jilly. She knew it would only be more of the same, with Jilly sensing something was up, urging Jane to tell her what, and Jane changing the subject. More half lies and evasions. No. She was better off just not going there.

Wednesday was about the same as Tuesday. Hope sprang up in the morning, at noon, and when she came home at night. Each time hope was crushed flat when she saw he was still gone.

Thursday came and went. She had her story hour in the afternoon. Even the beautiful, eager faces of the children didn't help much. She felt glum.

Bleak and empty.

Friday was the same. He didn't come home. He didn't return her call.

She called him again, late Friday night. Left a second message saying basically the same things she'd said in the first call. Only her voice was different. She could hear the change as the words escaped her lips.

She sounded sadder. And vaguely desperate. She hung up wishing she hadn't called.

By Saturday, she realized she was mad at him. Really mad. He was driving her crazy, staying away like this. Surely he must have some system for picking up his messages. He must know she had called him. Why didn't he call back? What was the matter with him? Had he no consideration at all?

Doubt began to gnaw at her. Maybe she'd read him all wrong. Maybe she hadn't hurt him at all. Maybe this was just the classic situation of a man getting what he wanted from a woman and moving on.

It felt awful, to think that.

But she did think it. How could she *help* but think it, with the way he was behaving, disappearing from her bed, from her house, from her *street?* Not returning her calls, gone for days and days…

She almost had a fight with her mother on Sunday. All morning, Virginia kept after her, nagging her. "Jane, is something the matter?" "You don't look well. Are you sick?" "You have circles under your eyes, honey. Aren't you sleeping well?"

Jane had given the usual answers. "I have some things on my mind." "No, I'm not sick." "And no, I haven't been sleeping all that well. But it's nothing for you to worry about."

"But what is it that I'm not supposed to be worrying about? And really, if you're not sleeping well, that *is* something for your mother to worry about. Sleep is very important. Sleep-deprived people can suffer all kinds of difficulties. Exhaustion can make a person careless. You could be in an accident. You could—''

It was right about then that Jane shouted, ''Mother, enough!''

Virginia subsided into injured looks and one-syllable remarks. Finally she left.

Jane had never been so glad to see her go.

Sunday afternoon, Jillian called. She'd gotten an offer to write a piece on Labor Day in the wine country. She wouldn't make it to the picnic after all. Jane told her she would be missed. And Jillian said that Jane sounded strange. Was something wrong?

Jane changed the subject and ended the call soon after that—and then felt glummer that ever.

Really, she did need to talk to someone eventually. She could use a little support. Maybe some good advice.

But every time she had the chance to bend a sympathetic ear, she turned it down. Why?

For some unknown reason, right then, she thought of Caitlin, remembered how she'd promised Cade's mother twice now that she'd get over to the Highgrade for lunch.

Tuesday, Jane left the bookstore at one-thirty. When she entered the Highgrade, the lunch rush was over. She found Caitlin at the register counter, looking through a stack of receipts. Cade's mother glanced up. A pleased smile lit up her face.

''Well, darlin'. It's about time.'' She came strutting out from behind the counter, all flash and fire and shimmering spangles. ''You come on with me. We'll get you a nice booth and I'll make sure you get your food on the double." She was already leading the way into the café.

And right then, Jane admitted to herself that lunch really was not what she'd come here for. "Caitlin…"

Cade's mother turned. One black eyebrow lifted. "What's up, sweet stuff?"

"I wonder, do you have a few minutes? Could we talk alone?"

Caitlin didn't even hesitate. "Why, sure. My office okay?"

"Great."

"Want a Coke?"

"I'd love one."

"Wait right there." Caitlin vanished into the café and returned a minute later with two tall red plastic glasses filled to the brim, and a couple of straws. "Here you go." Caitlin handed Jane her Coke and her straw. "Right this way." They went down the long central hall that led to the back parking lot. Caitlin ushered Jane through the second-to-last door on the right. "Have a seat."

The room was windowless and purely functional. There were metal file cabinets and metal shelves against the walls. A big green metal desk dominated the room, with a comfortable-looking leather swivel chair behind it. Two guest chairs faced the desk. Jane slid into one of them.

Caitlin went around the desk and dropped into the swivel chair. She cleared a space on the cluttered pad, peeled her paper off her straw and stuck the straw in her Coke. She sipped, long red nails gleaming as she held the straw. "Ah. Nothin' like a tall, cold Coke."

Jane sipped her own drink. "You're right. Thanks."

The two of them set their glasses on the desk at the same time. Then Caitlin leaned back in her chair. "Well, okay. What's goin' on?"

Jane's mouth went dry. She had one of those what-am-I-doing-here moments, a split second where she couldn't believe she'd come here, had no idea what in the world she wanted to say.

Caitlin sat forward again. Behind the false fringe of all those black lashes, her midnight eyes were shining bright. "Come on. It's okay, whatever it is. There ain't a thing you can say that I can't handle, honey-bunch."

All of a sudden, in the tilt of Caitlin's head and that gleam in her eye, Jane saw Cade, saw the resemblance of mother to son, though she had never really noticed it before. Cade was lean and rangy, with those silver eyes and that almost-blond hair. And Caitlin was all curves, with inky curls and eyes to match. But really, they were a lot a like. Smart and wild, the both of them. Determined to take life by storm, to live strictly on their own terms.

Jane said, "This is probably inappropriate, for me to be here, asking for your advice, but—"

"Is that what you're doin'? Lookin' for advice?"

"Yes. It is."

"And you don't really think I'm the right one to ask?"

"I only mean that you and I hardly know each

other. And then there's all that old stuff that happened, between you and my father.''

Caitlin picked up her Coke again and sipped from it. ''You know, I think sometimes that what happened way back when is never really gonna be known by anyone. Those of us that lived it, we each have our own version of it, all duded up and turned around to suit the lies we think we have to tell ourselves to get by.''

Jane leaned in. ''I do understand what you mean. We both know my mother, after all.''

Caitlin sipped more Coke. ''Your mother's not a very happy woman. Never has been. And I can tell you this much. I did not take your father to my bed. I promise you, I didn't.''

''Oh, I know you didn't. My aunt Sophie told me what happened.''

Caitlin chuckled. ''Miss Sophie Elliott. I always liked her.''

Jane smiled. ''Cade said he liked her, too.''

''Ah,'' said Caitlin softly. ''Cade did, did he?'' She looked at Jane steadily. Jane did not look away. Caitlin set down her glass and rested her hands on the arms of her chair. ''You're not really here to talk about what happened more than twenty-five years ago, are you?''

Jane swallowed. ''No. I'm not.''

Caitlin was frowning. ''You know, I told myself, that with you and Cade, I was going to stay out of it, that I would let you two work it out for yourselves.''

Jane wasn't quite following. ''With me and Cade?''

Caitlin cleared her throat. "Fact is I kind of messed it up, a little, between Aaron and the baby doll."

"The baby doll?"

"Your friend. Aaron's wife. Celia. I was gonna stay out of that, too. But I didn't. I had to get in there and do my bit. And what I did didn't help. But, well, you can see that they worked it out in the end. So no permanent harm was done. And this is a different situation, anyway, right? I mean, with Celia I kind of butted in. I went after her, tried to get her to let me help. But this time, you're the one comin' to me. Right?"

Jane still wasn't sure she was following. Still, she gamely replied, "That's right. I am."

Caitlin beamed. "You know, I gotta admit, it gives me a real charge, that you're here, that you see me as someone to talk to about this. Someone who is very much on your side. Because I am on your side. One hundred percent."

"Caitlin?"

"Yeah?"

"May I ask you something?"

"Shoot."

"Are you saying you know, about me and Cade?"

"Well hon, I'm not blind."

"So he hasn't…talked about me?"

"With *me?*" Caitlin waved her red-tipped fingers in front of her face. "I told you the other day. I'm just his ma. I look out for his place when he asks, I'm always here, if he needs me. But I don't get told a damn thing."

"Well, then how do you know that he and I—"

Caitlin swore under her breath. "Oh, come on. My vision's twenty-twenty. I see what goes on. I see the looks you two give each other, the kind of looks that could burn a buildin' down. Cade is crazy for you, and you're crazy for him. And whatever I can do to help you with that, well, here I am. Ready to do it. So drink that Coke and talk to me."

"I…"Jane picked up her Coke, then set it back down without taking a sip. "Oh, Caitlin…"

"Yeah?"

"You know about me—and about Rusty Jenkins?"

"I know you ran off and married him. That he was big trouble. That he put you through hell."

"Caitlin, I swore to myself I'd never make that kind of mistake again. But now, with Cade…"Jane's throat felt tight. And there was pressure behind her eyes. No way, she thought. I am not going to sit here and blubber like a baby. She gulped—to clear her throat, to force the tears down.

"With Cade, what?"

"Oh, Caitlin, he left. Out of nowhere. And now I miss him. So much."

"Well, of course you do. You love him."

Jane blinked. "I do?"

Caitlin only nodded.

Jane thought she ought to argue. But she didn't. She was thinking, is that it? Love? I love Cade….

The words echoed in her mind. They didn't sound so outrageous. Or incredible. They sounded kind of good.

Kind of like the truth.

And if they were the truth, well, what did that say

about her, about Jane Elizabeth Elliott, about how much she'd learned from the bad things that had happened to her?

"Oh, but Caitlin. Is there something *wrong* with me? All over again, I'm gone on a totally unsuitable kind of guy. I mean, ever since Rusty, I've been determined to be honest and straightforward and to find myself a straight-ahead guy. And what's happened? I end up in a one-night stand with my gambling, ladies' man next-door neighbor and now I'm carrying a torch for him." Jane shifted in the chair, suddenly angry. "And where *is* he anyway? Can anyone tell me? He's been gone for a week now, just locked up his house and vanished into thin air. Is he okay? Has he gotten himself into some kind of trouble?"

Caitlin was just sitting there, elbows on the arms of her chair, red-tipped fingers folded over her middle, listening. Watching.

Jane let out a hard breath. "Well?" She gestured, broadly, with both hands. "What? What do you think? What should I do?"

"If you'll shut up for a minute, I'll be glad to tell you."

Jane sank back in the chair. "Yes. All right. I'm listening. I am."

"Good." Caitlin waited.

Jane sat very still and didn't say a word.

Finally Caitlin spoke. "I could get real insulted, you know, at you comparin' my Cade to that loser, Rusty Jenkins."

Jane felt hot color rising to her cheeks. "I never

said that Cade was as bad as Rusty. I don't think that. Sincerely. I would never—''

''Jane.''

''Hmm?''

''Quiet.''

Jane pressed her lips together and nodded to show just how quiet she intended to be.

After a minute, Caitlin continued. ''I think you need to take a long, hard look at the facts here. My boy has not been in any real trouble in years. He's doin' damn well and I am proud of him. Yeah, he gambles. He gambles for a living. For him, it's a job. A job he likes. A job he happens to be damn good at. And as far as him bein' a player with the ladies, well, okay. Maybe he has been. The ladies like him. And he's always liked them right back—until the past year or so. Until he bought that house next to you. Since then, I haven't seen him look at any woman but the woman you see when you look in your mirror. Cade is…struggling now, searchin' for something more in his life than bright lights and a party all the time. He's come back home, he's livin' a decent life, trying to make a real place for himself.''

''But where *is* he?''

''Well, if I knew, I'd tell you. But I don't. And maybe that's not the question, anyway. Maybe what you should be askin' yourself is what you said or did that made him pick up and leave.''

''What *I* did?''

Caitlin gave Jane a long, knowing look.

Jane admitted grudgingly, ''Okay. Maybe you're right. Maybe it's my fault that's he's disappeared.

Maybe I said a few things I shouldn't have—or maybe I didn't say what I *should* have said fast enough. But couldn't it also be that you've read him wrong, when it comes to me? Couldn't it be that he's spent a night with me and that was all he wanted from me, so he's gone?''

"Oh, come on. Do you think that? Do you really think that?"

"Caitlin, I don't know what to think."

"I'll bet you don't. You're confused, aren't you?"

"That's right. I am."

"You don't know what to think. You don't know what to do. You are pretty much on the fence."

"Well, yes. That's right. I suppose I am."

"And that's most of your problem, the way I see it. One way or the other, you need to get off the damn fence. And all right, all right. I am no expert on the subject of true love. I've been married once—to a no-good murderin' bigamist, a child-stealin' con artist who lived a damn sight longer than he had any right to. Somehow, after Blake Bravo, I never felt up to tying the knot again. But I've seen a lot of what goes on in life. And I've learned that when it comes to love, *somebody's* got to go for it, to stand up and say, 'This is what I want and I'm gonna fight for it.'''

"And, in this case, that somebody ought to be me?"

Caitlin had to think for a moment before she answered that one. "Well, hon. Between you and Cade, it's hard to say. Sounds to me like neither of you really knows what you're doin' in this love affair of yours. But maybe, if you want my son to be with you for more than one night, you're gonna have to put in a little effort here. You're gonna have to show him that *you* want to be with *him*. You're gonna have to give him a few solid reasons why it'd be the smartest thing he ever did if he settled in on Green Street to spend his life with you.''

Labor Day dawned cloudless and warm, with the promise of a hot afternoon to come. At nine in the morning, Jane arrived at Wildwood Park, a rambling hundred acres of trees and grass, with a creek meandering through it. The park boasted a half-acre's worth of children's play equipment, a set of baseball diamonds and a large number of picnic areas, each with a table and benches and a barbecue consisting of a grated iron box on a fat steel post.

Jane went straight to the small stage that had been set up for her the day before. She had four half-hour segments planned. For each, she would read stories from the Brothers Grimm.

With a little help from a few talented parents, she'd created a three-sided backdrop with cottages and livestock and the occasional fairy and elf crouching in the underbrush in the foreground. Off in the distance, at the end of a winding road, stood a magical pink castle. The castle had a moat and drawbridge, banners flying and knights at the ramparts.

Jane had dressed to fit the theme. She wore a long sky-blue skirt and a white puff-sleeved blouse with a wide drawstring neck, a lace-up black leather corset over the blouse and black ballet flats on her feet. Her hair she more or less tamed into a pair of fat braids.

Privately she thought of the getup as Snow White meets the milkmaid.

The kids loved it. At ten, one and three, they sat spellbound as she read to them—rapt, yet always ready to shout the answers to any questions she threw their way. And between her performances, whenever they saw her hanging out with Celia and Aaron and all those visiting Bravos, they would wave and call out, "Story Lady! Hello, Story Lady!"

At her final 5:00 p.m. performance, she had an audience of about two dozen. She sat on a three-legged stool in front of the backdrop of cottages and castle. The kids crowded in around her, their parents watching, ranged in a semicircle a few yards beyond the children.

Jane read *Rumpelstiltskin* and *Snow White and Rose Red*. She was halfway through *The Frog King*, when she glanced up and saw Cade standing just beyond the semicircle of parents.

Chapter Twelve

Jane almost fell off her three-legged stool. Her heart seemed to stop in midbeat—and then started pounding again, way too hard, way too fast. He looked …eager. And tender, those silver eyes gleaming. And so *tan,* in a short-sleeved white shirt—unbuttoned, as usual—and a pair of loose cargo-style khakis, one of those Abercrombie and Fitch-style necklaces of wooden beads around his neck. He also looked…fine. Healthy. Unhurt.

She *had* been worried he might have got himself into some kind of trouble. But wherever he'd been, he'd come back in one piece.

It had been six days since Jane's conversation with Caitlin. Since then, she'd had a lot of time to mull over the things Cade's mother had said to her.

Jane had come to a few conclusions, after all that

mulling. Most important, that Caitlin was probably right on two counts, at least. That this just might be love. And that when it came to love, at least one of the two people involved had to go for it.

A smile trembled its way across her mouth. He smiled back. Warmth flooded through her.

One of the children, Elissa Lumley, who had a halo of frizzy red hair around her freckled heart-shaped face and an opinion on every story, chose that moment to tug on Jane's arm.

"Story Lady, the princess has to take the ugly frog back to her palace. Because he got her golden ball for her and she *promised.* A person *always* has to keep their promise."

The other children chorused agreement.

"Ah." Jane put on a serious expression and made a show of clearing her throat. "Well. Shall I read on and find out what happens?" She dared another glance at Cade.

He was gone.

Gone…

She nearly jumped from her stool, gathered up her sky-blue skirts and took off after him.

But no. Not now. In a few minutes. As soon as she'd finished up here.

Elissa still had her small hand on Jane's arm. The child wore a Barbie watch. It was 5:22. Eight more minutes, then, to the end of *The Frog King,* and the Story Lady could retire for the afternoon.

"Story Lady, did you hear us? We were all shouting, but you weren't edzackly listening."

Jane heard a chuckle or two from the ring of parents. They must have taken note of her reaction to the sight of Cade. Some of those parents were folks she'd known all her life, people who would be wondering out loud to each other about just what might be going on between Jane Elliott and the baddest of the bad Bravo boys.

A voice in her head—a voice that sounded a little like Caitlin and a little like her dear aunt Sophie—demanded, *Well so what? Let them wonder.*

That advice sounded pretty good to Jane.

She bent close to Elissa and spoke in a stage whisper. "Oh, I am so sorry. What did you say?"

"We said you should keep reading."

"Well, all right. I'll do that." She held the big storybook high and pointed at the picture of the beautiful, spoiled princess turning her back on the poor, ugly frog. "Oh, well what do you know? It looks as if the princess doesn't plan to keep her promise to the frog...."

About twenty minutes later, Jane found Cade sitting at a picnic table near the bandstand with Caitlin and Will. One of the big-time musical groups Aaron had managed to get for the picnic was well into a second set. People sat drinking beer and soft drinks from plastic cups and eating barbecued chicken and ribs slow-cooked in the big iron barbecue drums brought in on flatbeds for the occasion. Or they danced on the wooden dance floor that had been specially set up in honor of the day.

Jane caught Caitlin's eye and signaled with a lift of an eyebrow. Caitlin couldn't take the hint fast enough. All at once, she was standing, pulling on her second son's arm. Will got up and let Caitlin lead him away.

Jane moved in closer, until she was standing right behind Cade. There were people all around them. She knew that some of them were watching.

Well, okay. Let them watch.

Since she'd caught him checking out the Story Lady, he'd acquired a straw cowboy hat—along with a tall glass of beer. Jane stared at the back of his hat, not quite sure what to say to him, how exactly to begin.

The band finished the song it was playing. And Cade said, quietly, without turning, "What can I do for you, Jane?"

His tanned arm lifted. He drank from the cup. He still did not bother to turn around. If she hadn't seen his face, back there in the circle of grown-ups as she read to the children, she never would have guessed how glad he was to see her. He certainly didn't seem all that eager to turn around and talk to her now.

Jane moved in closer. She put her hands on his shoulders—oh, that did feel lovely, all that heat and lean, hard muscle. She had sincerely missed having her hands on him.

He stiffened—but at least he didn't pull away. The band started up again.

Jane bent close, breathed in the scent of his skin, and spoke into his ear. "Would you come for a walk with me?"

He turned his head then, slowly, and looked at her,

those silver eyes shaded by the brim of his hat. "People are watching, Jane."

She shrugged. "I asked you if you'd come for a walk with me. Someplace a little quieter. Where we could talk."

"Talk about what?"

The band was doing a very credible rendition of "Lady Marmalade." The lead singer, who wore a sexy dance-hall outfit and could belt it out with the best of them, kept the volume high. Jane was more reading his lips than hearing him. "It's too loud here. Please. Come with me...."

He took his sweet time making up his mind. But then at last he got up. She stood back so he could disentangle himself from the space between the picnic table and the bench. Once he was standing, he swallowed the rest of his beer and pitched the empty cup into a nearby trashcan.

She reached for his hand. He allowed her to take it, hesitating the tiniest fraction of a second before twining his fingers with hers. She stepped closer, and wrapped the fingers of her free hand around his arm.

He looked down at her with obvious suspicion. "What's going on, Jane?"

"We'll talk about that. This way." And she led him off into the trees.

Jane knew a place down by the creek, where the willows grew close and the loud music would be blocked by all the greenery and the steepness of the bank. It took them several minutes to get to it. They didn't speak the whole way. Jane didn't really care. Her hand was in his hand, she held onto his arm.

She was *with* him, at last, after two whole weeks of missing him, of longing for him, of thinking of all the things she should have done differently that final, beautiful night before he picked up and left. They saw people they knew, exchanged smiles and nods. Jane noted the knowing gleam in more than one pair of inquisitive eyes. Only a blind woman would have missed those swift looks of surprise, which were instantly followed by too-friendly smiles.

There would be talk, and lots of it, by the time the day was through. Jane would give them until tomorrow, at the latest. By then, someone would just *have* to tell Virginia Elliott who they'd seen holding hands with her only child.

A narrow path led down the bank to creekside. Jane half slid to the bottom, getting dirt in her little black shoes. Cade led the way, holding tight to her hand to help her keep her feet.

By the time they got to the water's edge, she was laughing. She stumbled and fell against him.

"Watch out." He caught her, his expression reluctant, his arms around her anything but.

She looked into his face and then she just couldn't help herself. She slid her hands up that hard chest and hooked them around his neck. "Oh, it's so good to see you."

He swore.

She grinned. She was pressed up close enough to know he was just as happy to see her as she was to be with him.

She sighed. "Listen. Please."

"What?" He growled the word as his eyes scanned her face, tracking from her mouth, to her eyes, to her nose, to the tip of her chin.

"I want you to take me out to Bennett's. How about tomorrow night? And as far as me telling my parents about us…"

"Yeah?"

"I don't think I'll have to. They'll know very soon. They might even know right now, the New Venice grapevine being what it is. They're both here today— not together, of course. But they're here. Someone is bound to tell them they saw us just now, holding hands, looking like a lot more than casual acquaintances."

He regarded her narrowly. "You're willing then, to have your mother know about me?"

"I am. And if her simply finding out isn't enough for you, I'll go further."

"Yeah?"

"I'll make a formal declaration of my intention to be seen in public with you on a regular basis. I'd do it this evening. However…"

"I knew it." He took off his hat, dropped it onto a nearby rock. "There's a catch."

"Um-hmm."

"Hit me with it."

"I'm hoping to be very busy this evening—all night long, as a matter of fact. So how about tomorrow? I'll give her a call and—"

Apparently he'd heard enough. His mouth swooped down.

Jane responded with utter abandon. She lifted her face to him, moaning aloud. Their lips met. Their tongues danced together and their bodies pressed close.

Oh, it was magical. The two of them, here in the moist coolness by the creek, hidden among the willows, kissing for all they were worth.

He lifted his head. She stood on tiptoe, to steal one more quick, mouth-to-mouth caress. Then she kissed his chin. And his neck. He nuzzled her throat, nibbled the hollow a little lower down.

And then, with a sigh, she went still, her head on his shoulder, enjoying the feel of his body against hers. She ran her fingers down his hard brown arm. "You're so tan...."

He chuckled. The sound echoed pleasingly against her ear. "One thing about livin' from hotel to hotel, there's always a pool to take advantage of between poker games. I swim. I sit in the sun. I use the gym. Believe it or not, I read."

"I believe it."

"And then there's my ongoing effort to improve my vocabulary. It's a life of endless excitement. Too bad we all know how I'll end up."

"How?"

"Busted. With a melanoma."

"Well, as far as the melanoma goes, you could try a little sunscreen."

"Doesn't fit my image."

"Put it on in your room. No one has to know."

"Hey. That's a thought."

"And as far as your ending up busted, well, who

says so? Caitlin tells me you're very good at what you do."

"You've been talking to Caitlin about me?"

"Yes, I have. Does that bother you?"

After a moment, he grunted. "Not really. She can drive Aaron up the wall, but she and I have gotten along pretty good in the last few years. We understand each other, I guess you could say."

"And Will?"

"What about him?"

"How does he get along with her?"

"Looks good on the surface. But who can say about Will? He's the deep one. Plays it close to the vest—and what did Caitlin tell you about me?"

"All good things."

"I'll bet."

She tipped her head back to meet his eyes. "You could have come home, right? Between those poker games."

"Yeah. So?"

She pretended to punch him in the arm. "So I missed you. A lot."

He frowned, but she could tell it was mostly for show. "Your signals were mixed the last time I saw you."

"I'm working hard on that."

"I've noticed." He was hiding a grin, she could see it. "And a homecoming like this is worth staying away for a long, long time." She shifted from one foot to the other. He frowned again. "What?"

"Dirt in my shoes." She stepped back enough to slip off one shoe and then the other, shaking them out in turn. He obligingly gripped her free hand, helping her keep her balance on the sloping bank. "There," she said, as she slipped the second shoe back on. "Much better."

He was looking her up and down. "Nice getup. Like something from an old Disney movie."

"That was the idea."

"I like the braids. They make you look so sweet."

"Don't kid yourself."

He chuckled. "Also, they make me think of *un*braiding them. And that lace-up thing. I *really* like that. And you know how I feel about little strings at the neck of your shirt. Very efficient."

"I am so glad that you approve of my costume."

The teasing light left his eyes. "So what happens now?"

She faked a look of surprise. "I get to decide?"

"Hey. I'm only the guy. We all know who runs the damn world."

"It's a relief to see you've come to understand the way things work at last."

"I'm not joking, Jane. What happens with us now?"

"Well, right now, I thought we'd go back to the picnic. Enjoy the evening. It's starting to cool off a little, which is nice. There will be dancing under the stars."

"You and me? Dancing? *Together?*"

"Exactly."

"More than one dance?"

"That's what I was thinking."

"This is what is called a breakthrough, right?"

She nodded. "We'll mingle. With your brothers and my best friend. With your mother and the Bravo relatives who came to town for this event. With my mother and my father, too, if we happen to run into them."

He winced. "Your mother."

"You can handle it."

He looked at her probingly. "You'll be with me. That's what you're saying."

"That is exactly what I'm saying. And then later…"

He had that part down. "We go home together."

"Yes. Where we can talk. In depth."

"And more than talk. In depth."

"Yes."

He had that look again—the glad one, the he'd had on his face when she glanced up and saw him while she read to the children. She knew her expression mirrored his.

He said softly, "I like it."

She grabbed his hat and held it out to him. "Well, then. Let's get started."

They danced. Repeatedly.

And they hung out with Cade's long-lost relatives.

Around seven, they loaded up a couple of plates and shared a table with Emma and Jonas Bravo. Jonas, who ran a multibillion-dollar corporation in L.A., liked to gamble for relaxation. He admired Cade's gold bracelet and asked Cade if he had any tips for a dedicated amateur.

Cade laughed. "The tips are always the same.

Don't bet what you don't have. Never draw to an inside straight. Know when it's time to get up and walk away—all the clichés. Which are clichés because they're true."

Emma Bravo, who was a successful businesswoman in her own right—not to mention gorgeous, with platinum hair and a sweet Texas twang—leaned Jane's way while the men talked gaming.

She confided that she and Jonas were expecting. "In April of next year." Emma patted her flat stomach. "I still can't believe it. Neither can Jonas. He says he's the happiest, luckiest man alive. I love it when he talks like that. Proves to me all over again that he is not the man I married."

Jane frowned. "*Not* the man you married?"

Emma laughed and leaned closer. "You should have known him before I married him and went to work on him. He was a mess. Well, I mean, emotionally a mess. To most of the world he looked like the walking definition of success. Rich as they come. Powerful. All that. But inside, he was lonely and unhappy. He wouldn't let anyone get close."

"What happened?"

"Love happened." Emma beamed. "I know it's corny, but love can do miracles. It truly can." Emma caught her husband's eye across the table. The look they shared brimmed with abiding affection—and considerable heat.

A few minutes later, Marsh Bravo, Cade's half brother from Oklahoma, joined them. His wife, Tory, was at his side, carrying their baby son Russell. Not far behind was their ten-year-old daughter, Kim and

Jonas's three-year-old adopted sister, Mandy, whom Jonas and Emma were raising.

Kim and Mandy had been to the face-painting booth.

"See me," said Mandy proudly, marching over to Jonas and holding up her small face. Fanciful, glittery flowers and butterflies perched on her cheeks and twined along her temples. "I am so beautiful."

"You are gorgeous," Jonas agreed. "You are absolutely dazzling." He grabbed her and tickled her and she squealed in delight.

After the meal, Cade led Jane out on the dance floor again. They swayed together to the music. Jane decided that right then, at that moment, she was the happiest she'd ever been her entire life—so far.

When the band took a break, they went back to sit down. Jane had barely settled at the table when Celia and Aaron appeared.

Celia marched right up and grabbed Jane's arm. "Come on. Right now."

"Ceil. What the—?"

"With me. Now."

Aaron let out a deep laugh. "She's a demon when she gets like that. You're better off to just do what she says."

Jane cast Cade a sheepish glance. He grinned and shrugged.

So Celia dragged her off to the baseball diamonds. They climbed the bleachers and sat in the top row, alone but for a few giggling teenagers a lot lower down.

"Now," said Jane. "What?"

"Oh, puh-lease. I don't believe this. I've been asking you what's wrong for weeks now. And you've been changing the subject on me."

"Ceil, listen—"

"Have you told Jilly?"

"About?"

"Oh, you know very well what."

She did know. And she also felt a little bit guilty for not telling her friends. "Cade."

"Duh."

"No, I haven't told Jilly."

"Well, that's something. At least I'm not the only one you don't trust."

"Ceil—"

"I'm hurt. I am. I trusted *you,* now didn't I? Back when Aaron hardly knew I existed? Back when I was sure he was never going to see me as anything but the best damn personal assistant he'd ever had the good sense to hire?"

"Ceil—"

"I told you—and Jilly—all about my hopeless case of unrequited love for the boss. I listened to your advice. And I took that advice. I don't necessarily expect you to do the same. But to *tell* me when I ask if something is bothering you, I do expect that. Especially from you, Jane. From Ms. Honesty-is-the-best-policy, Ms. Everything-starts-with-the-truth."

"You're right."

"I also—what?"

"I said, you're right. I should have told you."

"Well. Humph. At least you admit you were wrong."

"I was. I've been…confused."

"It's been going on for months, hasn't it?"

"If you mean the attraction between us, yes."

"Oh, I knew it. The minute I saw you with him today, everything fell into place. The way you'd always changed the subject whenever anyone asked about your new neighbor. The way you two would look at each other—and then look away."

"Yes. All right. All that did happen. But we weren't…together. We never spoke beyond the usual hi-how-are-yous."

"Until?"

"A few weeks ago."

"And? Oh, come on. Talk to me. You can spare a few minutes to bring me up to speed."

So Jane filled her friend in on the events of the past few weeks.

When she fell silent, Celia gaped at her in disbelief. "You talked to *Caitlin?* And it *helped?*"

"Yes, I did. And she was wonderful, really. She's a very smart woman."

"No argument there. She's smart as they come. But she wasn't any help at all to me. In fact, to be painfully honest, it was very much the other way around."

"She mentioned that."

Celia grinned. "But it all worked out in the end."

"She said that, too."

"And now, I adore my mother-in-law. She's one of a kind and I wouldn't trade her for the world—and you haven't said if you're thinking along the lines of Caitlin being *your* mother-in-law."

"You're right. I haven't said."

Celia pretended to pout. "And you're not going to, right?"

"How about if I keep you posted?"

"As if I have a choice. You'll tell me when you're good and ready, and we both know it. And I do hope you're not letting old garbage—that would be spelled *R-U-S-T-Y*—get in the way of things now."

"Maybe I was. But I'm not anymore."

"Good. Oh, Janey. I'm so glad to see you *glowing* like this. You're positively radiant. It's about time— and I just have to ask. About your mother…"

"She's not going to be a problem."

"You're sure?"

"I am absolutely positive. She can have all the fits over this that she wants. But in the end, she'll have to accept the fact that this is my life and it gets lived my way."

Chapter Thirteen

As the sunset faded and the first stars began to gleam in the darkening sky, Caitlin ordered the lighting of the paper lanterns that had been strung from tree to tree across the dance floor. Celia had brought along a new camera, a fully digital one. She took an album's worth of pictures. Jane and Cade were included in several of them, standing side by side, holding hands, grinning right into the camera.

"I want copies," Jane told her friend.

"Don't worry. You'll get them. Cross my heart."

Later, Jane and Cade took some time to wander over to the midway area across the creek. There was a Ferris wheel and a Tilt-A-Whirl, a carousel and a tunnel of love. With a toss of a coin, Cade won her a carnival glass fruit bowl.

They had their fortunes told by a gypsy who called

herself Madame Zuleika. She said the future looked bright, full of riches, of love and laughter—and babies, too. The fortune-teller did bear a strong resemblance to Mary Lou Garber, whose husband owned Garber's Hardware on Main. But neither Jane nor Cade let that bother them. They decided that when it came to predictions of good fortune, it didn't matter if a real gypsy—or the hardware store owner's wife—made them.

Jane hadn't seen her mother all day, and as the night drew on, she doubted that she would. Around ten, though, as she and Cade were once again swaying together on the dance floor, she spotted her father. Clifford Elliott, looking somber and aloof as always, stood with her uncle, the mayor, over by the Forest Service booth, where picnickers could get free posters of Sierra flora and fauna, as well as flyers on campfire safety.

Cade saw them, too. "Don't look now," he whispered in her ear. "But your father and my favorite ex-sheriff, J.T., are lurking over by the Forest Service booth."

"I know," she whispered back. "Don't be scared."

"You'll protect me?" He nuzzled the ear he was whispering in. "You won't let your uncle arrest me?"

She sighed and stroked the back of his neck with a fond hand. "I'll protect you. With my life." The song ended. She took his hand. "Come on."

He hung back. "Wait a minute. You're not planning to—"

"We should say hello."

"Jane..."

She looked at him from under her lashes. "Please?"

He muttered something that was probably profane, but then let her lead him off the floor.

Jane had inherited her stature and coloring from the Elliott side of the family. Her father was tall, with a deep chest and broad shoulders and dark hair now streaked with silver. Her uncle J.T. also had the dark, imposing look of an Elliott, with the same thick salt-and-pepper hair. But J.T. had always enjoyed a good meal. His stomach hung over his belt.

Her father saw them first. Jane had to give him credit. Except for an almost imperceptible narrowing of those dark Elliott eyes, her father gave no indication that the sight of his daughter with one of Caitlin's sons had any effect on him at all. Her uncle J.T. didn't dissemble quite so well. When he saw them, he scowled.

Cade muttered, "Are you sure about this?"

She sent him a smile, squeezed his hand and pulled him onward.

"Dad," Jane said brightly. "Uncle J.T. How are you two? Having a good time?"

Her father coughed officiously. And then he forced out a few words. "Hello, Jane. Yes. It's a beautiful evening. The picnic seems quite a success." He nodded at Cade—stiffly. But that didn't necessarily mean anything against Cade. Her father did a lot of things stiffly.

J.T. took his tone from his older brother, wiping

the scowl from his face and forcing a politician's smile. "Well. Yes. Ahem. Hello, you two."

Cade said, "Real nice to see you, Judge. You, too, J.T."

Jane asked, "So, Dad, have you seen Mom?" Cade squeezed her hand then. She got the message: don't push your luck.

He was probably right. But she felt reckless tonight. She felt powerful and bold—and strong in her determination to break down facades, to meet old demons head-on and vanquish them totally, once and for all.

Her father didn't miss a beat. He was, after all, a master of evasion when it came to questions about his wife. "Not recently, no."

"She did come to the picnic?"

Her father's mouth twisted in a sour approximation of a smile. "She always does, now, doesn't she?"

"Well yes, Dad. As a rule, she does. But I'm asking if you've seen her here, today. I mean, I know you didn't come with her, since the two of you never go anywhere together unless you absolutely have to, but still, maybe you—"

"Jane," Cade said. And that was all. Just her name. But the sound of it stopped her cold. She looked at him. He stared right back. She saw reproach in his pale eyes.

Her father said, quietly, "If I see her, I'll tell her you're looking for her."

Jane thought about the night ahead, the one she and Cade would spend at her house. She didn't want her mother interrupting them. "No. It's all right. Just tell her I'll give her a call tomorrow."

"I'll do that."

Cade wrapped it up. "Well. Great seeing you…"Jane's father and uncle nodded, and made a few more polite noises. Then Cade led her away to the booth where the beer was on tap in big steel kegs. "Beer?"

"Yes. Thanks."

He bought them the drinks and then led the way to a table under a big oak tree a couple hundred yards from the dance floor. They sat side by side, facing the distant bandstand and the dancers gliding in pairs under the golden glow of the paper lanterns. Cade set his hat on the table and took a long drink from his cup.

Jane sipped from hers. "All right," she admitted after a minute. "I went a little too far."

He slanted her a look. "That's right. You could find a better time and place to talk to your dad about his problems with your mother."

She looked into her beer. No answers there. "Sometimes I just get so tired of it, of the phoniness of it, the way that they live. I don't know how they stand it. I don't know how they—"

"Jane."

Morosely she sipped more beer. "What?"

"It's not your life. It's theirs. You're all grown up now and the way your folks live doesn't have a hell of a lot to do with you."

She knew he was right. "Sorry." She scrunched

up her nose. "I admit. I can be a little overbearing, now and then."

He faked a look of shock. "You? Never." Then he reached over to brush a loose strand of hair off her cheek. "Hey. It worked out all right. They took seeing us together pretty damn well, I thought."

She leaned a little closer. The oak tree shadowed them, made the picnic table seem a private place created for the two of them alone. "Yes. It did go well."

He leaned closer, too. "I have to admit, though, it was never your father I was worried about."

"Cade." Now she was whispering. Their faces were so close. Their lips almost brushed as they spoke.

"Yeah?"

"It's going to work out."

"You seem so sure."

"I am. After all, Madame Zuleika said so, didn't she?"

"Yeah. Yeah, I guess that she did...."

"I think you should kiss me."

"You know what? I do, too."

He moved that extra fraction of an inch. And their lips met.

The kiss started out sweet—and swiftly got steamy.

When they came up for air, he said, "I think it might be time to head on home."

They went to her house. She followed in her van behind the black Chevy extended cab pickup he'd bought because, he said, he was tired of the Porsche, that his legs were too long for it.

Inside, by the front door, on the long table where Jane had recently put a fresh arrangement of flowers in the mercury glass vase, they left a straw cowboy hat, Jane's small shoulder bag and the carnival glass fruit bowl.

Halfway up the stairs, on the landing beneath Aunt Sophie's portrait, they paused for a kiss—the kind of kiss that just never seems to end. By the time they moved on, they were both naked, their clothes strewn about on the stairs and the railing. Holding hands, they ran up the rest of the way and straight to the master suite.

They fell across the bed, laughing and eager. He tickled her and she tickled him back.

And then, he was over her, looking down at her. The nearly full moon poured silver light through the turret windows. His face was so still, so serious.

"What?" She touched his mouth, his cheek, stroked the line of his jaw. "Tell me…"

He laughed again, but it was a distant, self-mocking kind of sound. "I don't believe this."

"What?"

"I want you. I want to get inside you. I want to go over the moon with you."

"But?"

"I want to talk to you first."

She blinked—and then she laughed in pure delight.

He pretended to glare at her. "Oh, great. Laugh at me. Go ahead."

"I'm not. You know I'm not." She kissed the end of his nose. "I love that you want to talk to me." She squirmed out from under him and then turned on her side to face him, sliding a leg between his two hairy ones, cradling her head on her bent arm. "Okay. Talk."

"Well…"

"Hmm?"

"It's partly…why I left three weeks ago, and why I stayed away."

"Okay."

"I didn't even want to go."

That was lovely to hear. "You didn't?"

He shook his head. "I woke up and you were right there, beside me. And I only wanted to stay."

"But you left anyway."

"I was thinking that I had to get real, you know? That it wasn't going to work, with us. Not in the crazy, impossible way I'd suddenly realized I wanted it to work. That the problem with us was, I didn't know a damn thing about how to keep it going long-term with a woman. And you couldn't help me out with that because you didn't want to get anything going long-term with me."

Looking back on her own behavior that night, she could understand completely how he'd come to that conclusion. She made a small, sad sound deep in her throat.

"Hey," he said softly. "I'm not telling you this so you'll start beating yourself up."

"I know. I said what I said that night. I can't go back and do it over. But I also can't help wishing that I'd done it differently, that I'd been braver, bolder. More decisive, more what I always say I want to be— more honest."

He gave her a rueful grin. "You *were* honest. You'd made it clear from the beginning, what you were looking for in a man. And you'd told me that I didn't have what you were looking for—not by a long shot, not in my wildest dreams."

She let out a groan. "You know, I can't believe you stuck around for as long as you did."

"Where the hell was I gonna go? I was already gone. Long gone. On you."

"Oh, Cade…"

"It's all about irony, see? And yes, that was one of my words. At some point so long ago I couldn't say exactly when. Irony being…" He paused, his brow furrowed. And then he continued, reciting from memory, "Irony being *the incongruity between the actual result of a series of events and the normal or expected result*—and yes, incongruity was another word for another day.

"But back to irony. The way I get irony is, it's what happens when things don't turn out the way you'd think they would, given the way they've always turned out before. Irony can be pretty damn funny."

Jane spoke up then. "But not when it's happening to you personally."

"You got it. And the irony with us was that *you* were supposed to be the one who would want to make things permanent. *I* was the guy who would never, ever settle down—and more than that. Because for months and months, while I ached for you and thought that I was never going to get my hands on you, I kept telling myself that if I only could have you, just once, I would be all right. I would get over

you. It had pretty much always worked that way before—and yeah, all right, what that says about me
isn't so great. I've been with too many women and I
haven't been with any of them for very long.''

"So you always expect that it's not going to last.''

"Right. But I could tell, I knew, that night when I
woke up beside you. This time it wasn't going to turn
out the way I expected. I'd had you. And it was great.
And I wasn't thinking about moving on. I was thinking long-term. I mean, what the hell was that about?
I *never* think long-term. And you—when it came to
me anyway—were thinking anything *but* long-term.
You didn't want to be seen on a date with me. You
hoped you could keep your parents from finding out
what was going on between us.''

"Oh, Cade. I'm so sorry, about the way I acted
then. But now is not then. You know that, don't
you?''

He touched her chin with a finger and then kissed
her, once, a brush of a caress, his mouth to hers. "I
know. But I'm talking about that night, about why I
did what I did. I'm saying that waking up beside you
early the morning after was one of those lightbulb
moments. It hit me. I was going to get hurt. It was
only a matter of how much. I needed some time, to
think about the trouble I was in, some time to consider damage control. I had to go. Before you opened
those big brown eyes of yours and I started drowning
in them again. Before you touched me, before you
smiled at me, before you made me forget all the reasons I needed to get the hell out.''

"So you got the hell out.''

"Yeah. I did."

"Did you get my messages?"

"Yeah. It hurt me. To hear your voice. I wanted to come racing back here, to fall at your feet. I kind of despised myself for that."

"Why?"

"Oh, come on, Jane. You sound just like a woman."

"You men have way too much pride. And you did come back," she reminded him tenderly. "Finally."

"Yeah. I guess we both knew that would happen, too. That I'd be back. What I didn't know was that you had made a few decisions. The good kind of decisions, ones that went in my favor."

"I got help—from a very wise woman."

He laughed then. "Right. My mother."

"Don't laugh. Caitlin *is* wise."

"You don't know her like I do."

"What she told me was very wise."

"Maybe. And all right. I guess with all she's been through—and all the major mistakes she's made—she ought to be wise."

His lips were so soft. She had to kiss them again. She moved closer, pressed her mouth to his. He wrapped his arms around her and pulled her on top of him.

It was the moment, and she knew it. The moment to say it.

She lifted up just enough that she could look his eyes. "Cade Bravo, I love you. I am absolutely gone on you. I want you and only you, for the rest of my life. I want you so much. And I want…"

He smoothed her wild hair. "Yeah?"

She closed her eyes. "Oh, I shouldn't say this…"

"Yeah. You should. Come on. Say it."

So she did. "Your babies. I want that, Cade. A lot. I want children with you."

Chapter Fourteen

Babies.

It was a little more than Cade had bargained for. He knew a sudden and violent urge to jump from the bed and run down the stairs, grabbing his clothes from the landing as he went by, racing out into the summer night and away from this woman and all she offered—all she *demanded*—as far and as fast as his legs would carry him.

But then, if he did that, he would end up where he didn't want to be. Which was away from Jane.

She squirmed in his arms, rolling off of him and canting up on an elbow. "Oh, Cade. You're too quiet. I scared you, didn't I?"

He gave her a dark look. "You don't ask much, do you?"

"I did. I scared you."

"Jane. Come on. Don't you think this is all happening pretty fast?"

"Well, yes. I guess it is." She gave him a big, beautiful smile.

He looked at her sideways. "I mean, *babies?*"

"Yes, Cade. Babies."

"Right away?"

"Well, no…" He knew then, by the way she let that *no* trail off that *right away* was exactly when she wanted them. But she wasn't going to push that. "Not if you want to wait a while. I *will* wait. If you need more time."

He put his hand in her hair again, speared his fingers in it. He loved the feel of it. So warm and soft and *alive*. He captured a dark, twisting curl and guided it until it wrapped itself in a silken spiral around his finger.

He found he was thinking of what she'd always refused to tell him. Carefully he let loose of that curl, caught another one, guided it around his finger, too. "What's this about?"

Her dark brows had drawn together. "What do you mean? I was just telling you what I hope for. But if it's not what you want—if it's never going to be what you want—I'd like to know upfront, that's all."

"Is it really all?" He let that second curl go. "Is it everything you're trying to tell me?"

"I don't—"

"Look. You say you want babies—right away, if I'm willing."

"Yes. I do."

"But you haven't said if you can even *have* babies anymore."

She stiffened and jerked back. Those big dark eyes filmed over with sudden tears.

He felt like a thug, someone with no class at all. "Jane—"

"No." She swiped at her eyes with the back of her hand. "Don't apologize. You have every right to ask me that."

"But I could have done it in a better way."

"What better way? There is no better way. It's not your fault, what I did. What happened in the past. And the answer is yes. I *can* have babies. Or at least, the doctors *said* there should be no problem."

He wanted to touch her, to pull her close, to make it all better somehow. He reached for her.

"Wait." She put out a warding-off hand and scrambled to sit up. "I just...need a minute."

He did as she asked, keeping hands off, pulling himself against the pile of pillows at the headboard and keeping his mouth shut. He looked at her. That was always a great way to pass the time. She was so pretty in the pale moonlight. She'd grabbed a pillow and held it against herself, as if it could comfort her— or maybe, right now, she just needed some cover, to be a little less naked as she drummed up the courage to tell him the things she found so hard to say.

She sat with her legs crossed. Her hair fell in thick, untamed curls on her bare white shoulders. Her eyes were so troubled now. She clutched that pillow for all she was worth.

She sucked in a shaky breath and let it out fast. "I just…well, I'd like you to tell me—"

"Anything."

"How did you know?"

"Jane. Two and two generally adds up to four."

"But—"

"I know he beat you. I know you ended up in the hospital and lost your baby. It wasn't a big stretch to figure out what put you in the hospital."

"And there *was* talk, right? Back when it happened?"

"Yeah. I think I heard something. I don't remember what, exactly. Or who I heard it from." He put his hand on her knee, half expecting her to jerk away.

She surprised him. Her hand settled over his. For a moment, there was only that, the connection of touch. Then she pulled away and he let go, too.

She spoke in a small voice, holding that pillow to those beautiful breasts of hers, not meeting his eyes. "I'm still ashamed when I think of it. I like to imagine myself as strong, you know? A strong woman…"

"You *are* a strong woman."

She looked at him. And she swallowed. "I was five months pregnant. We had this fight. I don't even remember what started it. But at the end of it, after he'd hit me in the face a few times, he shoved me backward. I landed on the floor. I turned over, as quick as I could, tried to curl into myself, to protect the baby. But he just circled around me. He kicked me in the stomach."

Cade thought it was probably a very good thing

that Rusty Jenkins was already dead. "And you lost the baby."

She nodded, swallowed again. "He walked out. I managed to crawl to the phone and dial 911. They came and took me to the hospital—and yes. There were questions. Suspicions. On the part of my parents, of Celia and Jilly, of Aunt Sophie and the nurses and my doctor. Reports were filed. But I wouldn't admit it, wouldn't say what he'd done to me—and more important than me, to our innocent baby. I was too afraid of him. I knew better than to tell what he'd done. I knew that if I told, he would find a way to get to me. A way to hurt me and hurt me bad."

"So you said nothing."

She nodded again. "And then the time came when it didn't matter anyway. Rusty was dead. It was over, all in the past."

"Good," he said flatly.

"Was it? I don't know. Yeah, he was gone. And I didn't have to live in fear of him. But it was also too late, you know?"

"Too late for…?"

"To stand up to him, to make him face a few consequences for what he'd done. He was dead. There was no need anymore to tell anyone. A dead man has no consequences left to face."

"You're saying your parents never knew?"

"Oh, they knew. They guessed. But I never told them outright."

"You never told *anyone* outright?"

"No. I did tell. Eventually. I don't think I could have gotten over it, could have gotten on with my life, without getting it out, without talking about it to people I could trust. I was in counseling for a while. My counselor knew. And Aunt Sophie. And Celia and Jillian, I told them, a few years ago. I…well, I always planned to tell the man I married.''

He smiled at that. ''Right. That steady, solid, dependable guy.''

She gave a low, sad little laugh. ''Yeah. That one.''

He reached out, took the satiny edge of the pillow she held and gave it a tug. She let it go. He tossed it over his shoulder. And then he held out his hand to her.

With a small cry, she came to him. He pulled her in, guiding her down, tucking her against him spoon-fashion, so he could wrap his arms around her and bury his face in all that dark, sweet-smelling hair.

She let out a long sigh. ''It's the worst regret in my life. That I didn't stand up to him. That only the accident of his death set me free of him, gave me a chance to start over.''

He stroked her hair, her shoulder, the long, soft curve of her arm. ''It happened like it happened. But don't sell yourself short. You would have found a way. To face him down. To get free of him.''

''Maybe. But I'll never know for sure.''

He whispered, ''Hey.''

''Um?''

''Forget the regret. You're alive. He's not. And the way I heard it, he more or less engineered his own death, with that stupid botched holdup attempt. He got what he deserved. And you didn't have to risk his murdering you to make it happen.''

"I didn't stand up to him."

"Jane."

"What?"

"Sometimes the cards go against you. Sometimes you don't have a prayer. You've got a losing hand. So you fold. You let it go."

"But I—"

"Jane. Let it go."

She made a noise of reluctant agreement. He pulled her in closer, resting a hand against her belly, then moving it upward, to cup one full breast. She sighed, snuggling her bottom up closer, making him all the more acutely aware of what he wanted to do to her.

Very soon now.

He smoothed her hair out of the way, kissed the tender skin on the side of her neck.

It was all like some dream, in a way. Coming home, expecting that the best he was going to get from her was a lot of sneaking around and maybe a few more bouts of great sex.

And instead…this.

An evening right out in the open, the two of them, side by side. The truth about that SOB, Rusty, at last.

Her telling him she loved him. And wanted his babies.

Love.

Now there was a hell of a concept.

Was that it, what he felt for her?

How would he know, for certain? How could he say?

He knew he was…looking. Had been for a while

now. Trying to find something solid. Something that would last.

And with her, he did feel something different than ever before. A deeper kind of wanting. A sort of hopefulness for the future.

But could it really last, like she said, for their whole lives?

"Jane?"

"Hmm?"

"About you and me…"

He could feel the sudden stillness in her. "Yes?"

"I…well, I'm willing, all right? To give it a try."

She started wiggling then. He supposed he'd known she would. She wouldn't stop until she'd turned over and could look into his eyes. She stroked a hand down the side of his face. "Give what a try, Cade?"

"You and me. The baby thing."

"Ah." She ran the back of a finger along the line of his jaw. "The baby thing…"

He reminded himself that there was something he'd better make clear to her before those wonderful hands moved any lower. "Listen."

"Mmm?" Her eyes were dreamy.

Too dreamy. "I mean it. There's something I want you to understand."

She blinked. "Okay."

"You know the story, of my father. Met my mother when she was seventeen, supposedly married her, gave her three sons—then faked his own death in an apartment fire, disappeared from our lives. Went off to do a lot of evil and illegal things."

"Yes. I remember. I've heard all the stories."

"The key word is *supposedly*."

Her eyes changed as understanding dawned. "Are you saying that Blake Bravo never actually married your mother?"

"You got it."

"But she had three children with him."

"That's right. And we have our suspicions about that, my brothers and me."

"Suspicions?"

"Yeah. The only thing we can figure is that she kept having babies to try to force him to marry her."

She sat up. "Oh, no. Not Caitlin."

That made him chuckle. "Why not Caitlin?"

"Well, because. Caitlin makes her own rules and doesn't let anyone tell her how to live her life. She would never do something so calculating, just to get a man's ring on her finger."

"Jane. You don't know my mother as well as you think you do."

"Oh, please. I just can't buy that she would do that. And not only because it's so manipulative, so scheming."

"Caitlin can be manipulative, Jane."

"But it's *pitiful*, too. She had to have seen the hopelessness of it. I mean, if he didn't marry her after Aaron, what made her think he would after Will—or you?"

"Good question. But then, we're talking about Caitlin. Most of the time, her motives are a black hole to the rest of us."

"I'm sorry. I still can't believe she would—"

"Jane. Face it. She just might. You can't let your-self get too carried away with some fantasy idea about my mother. She's no angel. And she never has been. And whatever her reasons for having Blake Bravo's kids without having his ring on her finger, she did it."

"But…she's Caitlin *Bravo*. That's been her name as long as I can remember."

"Eventually she just started calling herself that, and after a while, it stuck. And she gave my brothers and me his last name when she filled out the birth certificates. So yeah, we really *are* Bravos. But the fact is, Caitlin McCormack and Blake Bravo never officially tied the knot. And folks called us *those bad Bravo boys* and also *those little Bravo bastards*. In both cases, what they called us was the truth."

Her eyes were soft with sympathy. "Oh, Cade. I'm so sorry. I always thought it was…just an expression, you know?"

He hooked his hand around the back of her neck and brought her sweet face down to his. "Here's an-other truth for you, Jane. If you had some idea about being the single mom of my baby, get over it. I'm not bringing any bastards into this world. You get my drift?"

"I…yes. Well, of course. I don't want that, either. Honestly I don't."

He let go of her then. He hauled himself to a sitting position and pulled out the drawer in the nightstand by his side of the bed. As he'd expected, the remain-ing condoms from that other night were there. He took one out. "Say what you want about all the women I've been with. One thing I've always done right.'' He shoved the drawer shut and held up the little foil pouch. ''And that's *not* getting anyone pregnant.'' He saw the gleam in her eyes then. And he knew what she was thinking. ''Go ahead. Say it.''

''What about Enda Cheevers?''

He glared at her. ''What about Enda?''

''Well, everyone says—''

''You know, I hate that. What everyone says. Did it ever occur to you that what everyone says might not be true?''

''Cade, I'm only—''

''I don't give a damn what people say. That baby of Enda's wasn't my kid. If you think back, maybe you'll remember how she left town not long after the incident between me and her daddy and her daddy's shotgun.''

''Yes. I remember.''

''She ran off with the baby's father, an encyclopedia salesman from Bend, Oregon.''

''Oh,'' Jane said. He could see she was embarrassed at how eagerly she'd believed all the rumors. Good, he thought. She ought to be embarrassed.

He said, ''I've never done what my daddy did. And I never will. I'm not givin' any small-minded people an opportunity to call an innocent kid a damn ugly name.''

She was looking at him sideways, kind of nervous—and kind of hopeful, too.

He caught her hand, turned it over and set the condom in her palm. ''So it's your choice.'' He curled her fingers over it. ''We use that. Or we don't. If we do, well, that's okay. We can take a little time, to be sure about all this, before we jump right in to having a family.''

"And...if we don't use it?''

"Then you get a chance at what you say you want. My baby. And you marry me. Tomorrow.''

Damn. Had he really said that?

Apparently yes, judging by the dazed expression on her sweet face. She stared for an endless two or three seconds—and then she let out a sharp, surprised laugh. "*Marry* you?''

He wondered if he should be insulted. But no. He couldn't blame her for being surprised. He was pretty stunned himself at what had just come out of his mouth.

"Well,'' she said.

"Well, what?'' It came out sounding gruff.

A big smile broke across that mouth he always longed to kiss. "Well, great. Works for me.''

He frowned. "That was a yes, right? I mean, is that a yes?''

"Of course it is.''

"You're sure?''

"I am. This is exactly what I want.''

"It is?'' It occurred to him right then that they were both stark, raving nuts. He couldn't believe what he'd suggested. And she should damn well have had sense enough to hesitate, at least.

But she wasn't hesitating. Far from it. Her eyes were shining—and not with tears. "Oh, yes. It's just what I want—what I didn't quite dare to propose my-self. Oh, Cade. You are so much braver than I am.''

"Uh. I am?"

"Yes. Oh, yes. You are." She tossed the condom over her shoulder.

He watched it go flying. It hit the nightstand on her side of the bed, bounced off and dropped to the floor. "Hey. Get serious, Jane. Are you *sure?*"

"Yes. I am sure."

"But—"

She threw her arms around him, pressed all those womanly curves and hollows against him. "No buts. We're doing this. Too late to back out now."

"I can't think when you do that."

She tipped her head back and grinned at him. "When I do what?"

"Throw yourself on me, all naked like that."

"Well, good. Don't think. Just kiss me and make love to me and forget about everything but how good it feels."

He grabbed her waist in both hands with the idea that he would push her away a little. Bright move. Once he had a hold of her, there was only one option: to pull her closer. "Damn you, Jane."

"Are you getting cold feet on me?"

"I'm not what you wanted. I'm not—"

"Oh, yes. You are. You are just what I wanted. What I've needed. What I've been looking for. I know that now."

He had to admit, he liked the sound of that. "Me? You've been looking for *me?*"

"Yes, I have. And you know that other guy—that nice, steady, dependable guy? The guy I never found?"

"Yeah?" He wasn't sure he wanted to talk about that guy. But he asked anyway, "What about him?"

"I never found him because I never *wanted* to find him. Because he wasn't for me."

Well, all right. This *was* getting interesting. "How do you figure that?"

"He wouldn't have been good for me. And I certainly wouldn't have been good for him. We would have bored each other silly."

"Oh, yeah?"

"Yeah. Because I have this tendency…"

He stroked his hand down the full curve of her hip. He couldn't help himself. Her body held endless enchantments. Just to look at her, to touch her, to feel her quiver beneath his hands….

She moaned.

He gave her train of thought back to her. "You have this tendency…"

"Ah. Yes. I do. A tendency to play it safe. To get stuck in a rut. To be stodgy and self-righteous. To be humdrum."

"Humdrum. As in boring?"

"That's it, that's what I said."

He definitely did like the way this conversation was headed. "And that means you need…"

"…someone to shake me up a little, someone to remind me that life is not only safety. There has to be risk. Adventure. Chances taken."

He cupped her bottom. It was a beautiful bottom. Fit just great into his hands. He bent enough to nibble on the tender curve where her shoulder met her neck.

She made a small sound of surprise and delight. Then she said, with enthusiasm, "Oh!"

"Lots of deep thoughts going on here, Jane."

"Oh, yes. If I can only…"

"What?" He sucked on that soft, white skin.

"Remember…"

"Yeah?"

"What I was talking about…"

He lifted his head, just enough to note with satisfaction the love mark he'd left at the base of her throat. He touched it, rubbed it, with his thumb. "You said there has to be risk."

She moaned some more. He really liked that. Hearing her moans.

"Yes," she whispered, breathless. Sighing. "That's right. Risk. I think—" She gasped as he caught her earlobe between his lips, worried it, then lightly nipped it with his teeth.

He reminded her, "You were saying?"

"Mmm…"

"You said, you think…"

"Yes. I do."

"You think *what?*"

"That there was a reason I fell for Rusty."

"Rusty," he muttered, running his tongue along the ridge of her collarbone, "should burn in hell."

She groaned. "I try not to judge him."

"Well, I'm not that noble, Jane. I judge him. And I say he should burn in hell."

"Well—oh!—that's how you feel. I can't tell you how to feel."

"That's right."

"But I mean—" She cut herself off with another of those sweet moans of hers.

"You mean what?"

"Well…" She caught his mouth, kissed it, then started talking again. "It was all wrong—"

"What?" He asked the question—then tried to catch her mouth again.

She canted her head back, avoiding his kiss in order to answer. "Between me and Rusty, it was all wrong. Rusty was in no way the right man for me. But I see…an important urge there."

"An urge."

"That's right." She brought a hand between them and traced his lips with the pads of her fingers. "Such a beautiful mouth…"

"What about this urge, Jane?"

"This urge?"

"With Rusty. You said there was an urge. An important urge."

"Ah. Right. It was an urge to…take chances. To invite a little risk."

"A *little* risk?" He dipped his head and ran his tongue down her throat.

"Okay." She grasped his shoulders, made a low, purring sound. "I went overboard. I was seventeen, when it started with him. My life was so…locked up. I felt hemmed in, on a treadmill, everything gray and dull. I saw my life stretching ahead of me, antiseptic and constructive, with no excitement, no *fun.*"

He lifted his head and met her eyes. "Because of your parents?"

She nodded. "Especially my mother. Her expectations for me were crushing me. Their life together was a lie. I wanted to be free of them. With Rusty, I broke out.''

''Yeah, in a big way.''

''I *said* it was all wrong. Rusty ended up being the wrong risk, a bad chance I never should have taken. He killed our baby. He almost killed me. But the basic urge—the urge to break out, to play it some other way than safe—I think I was onto something there.''

He considered her words for a moment, and decided they made sense. ''Okay. I see what you mean.'' Her lashes fluttered down. He caught her chin in his hand and tipped it up to him. ''Jane...''

''Mmm?''

''We've been talking, Jane. We've talked a lot.''

''Yes, we have.''

''I'm kind of tired of talking now, for a while. Okay?''

''Oh. Yes. That's fine.''

''You gonna kiss me now, Jane—some slow, long, deep kisses? You gonna let me kiss you back?''

She licked her lips. He figured that was answer enough. He guided her down among the pillows as he covered her mouth with his own.

Chapter Fifteen

Late in the night, Cade woke.

His first thought was a question: What am I doing here? But then he looked over and saw Jane sleeping, her face soft and defenseless as the babies she said she wanted to have with him.

Looking at Jane, he found himself thinking it would be all right. They would make it, somehow. She really did seem sure that he was what she wanted, that what they could build together would be something worth having.

For the most part, he agreed with her. He had this feeling of rightness, when he was with her. This feeling that the world was a better place than he'd known it to be before he found her. That there were more possibilities than he'd realized. That with Jane, he'd always be looking forward to coming home. And that he wouldn't ever be lonesome when he got there.

There was going to be a lot to deal with, though. Like how she would handle it when her mother cut her off again. And he didn't kid himself. Virginia Elliott was going to go seriously sideways when she found out her daughter had hooked up with another bad boy. And not just any bad boy. Uh-uh. Much worse. This time, Jane had picked herself a bad boy with Bravo for a last name.

And then he couldn't help asking himself, was Jane really ready to marry a guy who didn't pull a nine-to-five? A guy who took off for days and sometimes weeks at a time in order to bring home the bacon? A guy whose income could be spotty, to put it mildly?

Did she really want to have her babies with a guy like him?

Jane stirred. She yawned. She looked so cute when she did that. He felt her soft hand, reaching for him under the sheet.

She found him.

He pushed his doubts to the back of his mind and moved into her waiting arms.

They got up at daylight. Cade headed for the shower and Jane went downstairs, to get the coffee started and to collect their clothes from the stairway.

A few minutes later, she joined him in the shower stall. They stayed in there until the water turned cold.

Downstairs at a little before eight, Jane scrambled some eggs and he made the toast and they sat at her breakfast table with the morning sun pouring in the bay window, sipping coffee, talking about their wedding—or more accurately, *she* talked about their wedding. He listened and he agreed, happy just to watch her as she made her plans. Her face had a glow about it. And the morning sun made her hair shine, catching those hints of brown and red in the dark strands.

She still seemed sure—that she wanted to marry him and that she wanted to do it that day.

"I need to go over to the bookstore," she told him. "I've got to make a few arrangements with my clerk. And I want to call Jilly. And Ceil, too—I think she said she and Aaron were staying in town until this afternoon. And I want to talk to my mother."

Cade knew a few bad words he wouldn't have minded muttering about then. He held them back. He picked up his coffee mug and saluted her with it. "That'll be interesting." He sipped.

The happy glow had left her face. She looked bleak. And determined. "It has to be done. Yes, this is sudden. But I want to make it very clear to everyone. We're proud and we're happy and we're not sneaking around. I'll call her right after breakfast and tell her that we're getting married."

He set down the mug. "Hold on a minute."

She stiffened in her chair. "Why?"

"Think twice."

"About what?"

"Your mother's not going to like this."

Her lips flattened out. "Too bad. It's not her choice to make."

"Hey," he said softly. "Relax. I'm on *your* side."

She raked a hand back through all that gorgeous

hair. "I just don't think we can afford to back down when it comes to her. Sooner or later, she's going to have to accept our marriage."

"No, she's not. It may be our choice to get married. But it's her choice how she deals with it."

"Whatever. We *are* in agreement that there's not going to be any sneaking around, right?"

He gave her a nod.

She gestured, emphatically, with both hands. "So then, one way or another, my mother is going to hear about our marriage. And I think it's important that she hear it from me—and before the fact."

"I'm not arguing."

That shut her up. For about half a second. "You're not?"

"No. I'm just saying you should tell her to her face. Not on the phone, not unless you have no other choice."

She finally caught on. And she looked damn sheepish. "You know, you're right. I'll call her. Say I need to see her right away. How's that?"

He couldn't help smiling. "Sounds good to me."

"Oh. And my father. I'll call him, too—I think that's acceptable, that I tell him over the phone. Don't you?"

"Sure."

"And we can't forget Caitlin. You'll call her, won't you?"

"Be glad to."

"Anyone who wants to come, fine. We can caravan."

"You know that means Caitlin for sure, don't you?"

"No problem. I'd love to have your mother at our wedding."

"Fair enough. And I'll see if I can get hold of Will."

"Yes." She leaned across the table and kissed him. She smelled of coffee and Ivory soap. Wonderful smells. He couldn't get enough of them.

She dropped back into her chair and sipped from her mug again. "I can be ready to go by eleven. Is that okay?"

"It's good with me."

"How about Tahoe?"

"Fine."

"We'll be there in no time. We'll get the license and then we'll find the nearest chapel."

He laughed. "This is what they mean when they say a hasty wedding, right?"

"Oh, maybe. I don't know. I don't care. I only know that before tomorrow comes, we'll be married. And I'm glad."

He held out his hand.

She reached across and took it. "We'll just come on home, after the ceremony. Is that all right with you?"

"It's fine with me."

"Maybe in a few weeks—whenever we can both spare the time—we'll plan for a wedding trip."

"I'd like that."

"Oh, Cade. We're going to be very happy."

"You sound pretty damn certain."

"I am. I truly am."

* * *

The doorbell rang as they were clearing up the breakfast dishes. Jane knew who it would be.

Cade seemed to know, too. He grabbed the dish towel and dried his hands. "Listen. I'll go out the back, all right? You talk to her, break it to her as easy as you can manage it. She could have a damn heart attack, if the first thing she sees when she walks in your door is me."

Jane knew he had a point. It would probably be better if she talked to her mother before Virginia actually saw them together.

But then again, why cater to her mother's sad, sick little prejudices?

"She'll live," Jane said, closing the dishwasher, taking the towel from him to dry her own hands. "And remember, the whole idea here is that we're not going to sneak around."

The doorbell rang again.

"I don't like it," Cade said. "You should talk to her alone first, tell her what's going on. Give her that much. I'll just go to my place. You bring her over there if and when you think she can handle the sight of me."

She hung the towel on the hook beneath the cabinet. "It's not right, Cade. Listen to yourself. *If and when she can handle the sight of you?* I hate that. That's not fair to you."

"Yeah, well. Where was it that you got the impression life was gonna be fair?"

"But—"

"Look. All the time I was growing up, there were big scenes. Big confrontations. Caitlin screaming and the three of us shouting right back at her. They did nothin' for nobody. Just made raw edges, you know, the next time we rubbed up against each other. Why ask for that if it's not absolutely necessary? Why not cut your mother as much slack as we can afford to in this? Over time, maybe, she'll get used to me. I'm not counting on it, but I'm hoping. I don't want to give her any excuses to hate me any more than she already does. I want to know that we did what we could, that we broke the news to her in the most gentle way possible."

She stared at him, thinking what a good man he was—at heart, where it really counted. No wonder she loved him. And maybe he was right. And even if he wasn't, they couldn't stand here all morning debating the issue. "Okay," she conceded. "I'll talk to her first—if it is actually my mother at the door."

Again, the bell rang—three times in succession—insistently, impatiently.

"It's your mother," said Cade flatly.

"I'll bring her over to your house in a few minutes."

"I'll be there." He turned for the door to the service porch.

It was her mother all right. And she was fuming. Jane could see her through the beveled glass in the top half of the front door. Her eyes were narrowed, her mouth pinched up tight, her back ramrod-stiff.

Someone must have already told her that Jane had spent last evening at Cade Bravo's side.

Jane slid back the dead bolt and pulled open the door. Her mother grabbed the outer door, yanked it wide and stepped inside.

"Jane." Virginia Elliott made the name both an accusation—and a rebuke.

"Hello, Mother." Jane brazened it out by forcing a pleasant tone.

Her mother didn't bother with pleasantries. "Jane, I have heard the most…well, I don't know what to say. I just—"

"Mom. I'm glad you came over."

"What? Glad? I don't—"

"I have the coffee made. Come on back to the kitchen." Jane put her arm around her mother's thin shoulders and attempted to shepherd her down the central hall.

"I don't want…" Right then, Virginia caught sight of Cade's hat on the long table. "Whose hat is that?"

"Mom—"

Virginia jerked free of Jane's guiding arm. "I asked you a simple question. You can just answer it. Whose hat is that—there, on that table?" Virginia blinked. "And that vase? That strange golden vase. You would never tell me who gave you that vase. I think you should tell me now."

Jane stepped back. She felt regret—mostly for Cade's sake. He'd wanted her to handle this delicately. But there was just no way to do that. Her mother was irrational in her fury. And it was only going to get worse.

"Tell me," Virginia demanded. "Tell me now."

Jane made one last try. "Are you sure you wouldn't like a cup of coffee?"

"Stop babbling about coffee. I have no interest in coffee. Is that Cade Bravo's hat on your table there? Did he give you that vase?"

Jane drew in a long breath and let it out with care. "Yes," she said. "Right on both counts. It's Cade's hat and the vase was a gift from him to me."

"Oh, my God," said her mother. "Oh, my sweet Lord."

"Mother—"

"Everyone is talking, you know. Lotty Borghesian. And Edna Reese. They both called me. I didn't believe it. How could I believe it? I told myself, Jane wouldn't do this, Jane wouldn't be so foolish, not now. That's all behind her, all that craziness over the wrong kind of boy."

"Mom. I'd really appreciate it if you'd settle down, if you'd pull yourself back from the brink."

The veins in Virginia's neck stood out in sharp relief. She wasn't wearing her pearls so she couldn't fool with them. Instead she clutched her thin hands to fists at her side. "Settle down? Pull myself back from the brink? What are you talking about? What is going through that mind of yours?"

"What is going through my mind is that I hope you don't take this too far. I hope you don't say anything I'll find too hard to forgive."

"You hope *I* won't say anything *you* can't forgive?"

"Yes, Mother. That's what I said. I'm so sorry, that

you have this…obsession with Caitlin Bravo and anyone related to her. But I can't and won't live my life
by your obsessions. I am in love with Cade Bravo.
And I'm marrying him. Today."

Virginia gasped as if she was having trouble getting
enough air. "What? Today? You can't be serious."

"Oh, but I am. We're getting married in Tahoe this
afternoon. You're welcome to come, if you promise
to behave yourself, to treat Cade—and his mother and
his brothers—with respect and courtesy."

Virginia groped her way backward. She reached the
chair by the entrance to the front room and slowly
lowered herself into it. All the outrage seemed to have
left her. Now she looked horrified, crushed. And desperate.

"Jane." She leaned forward, all urgency. "You
can't do this. You can't ruin your life a second time.
Oh, what is the matter with you? There have been
nice men, in your life. *Good* men."

"Mother. Cade *is* a good man."

Virginia waved her hand as if batting off flies.
"What happened to that science teacher? He was a
fine—"

"Mother. Get it through your head. I'm marrying
Cade. Today."

"Oh, that's impossible. You *can't.*"

"I can. I am."

"Oh, my Lord. Oh, no. Oh, please. Cade Bravo is
Rusty Jenkins all over again. You have to see that.
You have to see that you have a real *problem* here,
when it comes to men, that you have some…fatal

weakness, for the wrong kind of man. You're not able to—''

A fatal weakness? It was enough. It was way too much. ''Mother.''

''Oh, Janey. Oh, honey…''

''I want you to listen to me.''

''Jane—''

''No. Stop.''

''You simply cannot—''

Jane put up a hand. ''Are you listening?''

''But I have to make you—''

''Stop.''

''I have to—''

''Stop!''

Her mother made a whimpering sound, then started to speak again.

Jane didn't allow that. ''Not. Another. Word.''

Virginia drew in a ragged breath, shut her mouth, and nodded.

Jane said, slowly and clearly, ''I love Cade Bravo. He is not Rusty Jenkins all over again. And if you were capable of looking at this situation reasonably, you'd see that he's not. I said it once and I'll say it again. I'm going to marry Cade. Today. I spoke too hastily, I realize, in inviting you. You're *not* welcome at my wedding, Mother. I love you, but you'd only make trouble. And I just don't need that. Not today.''

''Oh, Jane.'' Her mother stood and reached out pleading arms. ''Don't do this.''

Jane stepped back. ''Go on home now, Mother. I have a lot to do this morning. It's my wedding day.''

Chapter Sixteen

Jane stood on her porch and watched her mother drive away. Then she went over to Cade's.

He had the door open before she got all the way up the walk. With a small cry, she ran to him. He met her on the top step, enfolding her in his strong arms. She hugged him tight, pressing her face into the side of his neck, feeling his morning beard, rough against her cheek. He rocked her gently, from side to side, holding on as tight as she was.

Finally she pulled back.

He asked, "Not so good, huh?"

"Disaster. But then, I guess I knew it would be."

He lifted an eyebrow at her. "Are you trying to tell me that your mother won't be coming with us to Tahoe?"

"I told her I didn't want her there."

"Ouch." He guided an unruly curl of hair away from her mouth. Then he took her hand and pulled her down with him, to sit on the steps. "What did she say, exactly?"

Jane gave him a wry look. "Are you sure you want to know?"

"Good point. Forget I asked."

She leaned her head on his shoulder. They were quiet for a moment, just sitting there on his front step, staring down his front walk. Above them, the sky was clear and blue. Not a cloud in sight.

Finally he said, "Maybe someday…" And then he didn't seem to have the heart to finish the sentence.

She braced her elbow on her knee, cupped her chin in her hand and looked up at that gorgeous blue morning sky. "Well. One good thing."

"And that is?"

"I love you, and it's a beautiful day for a wedding."

"That's two things."

"Yeah, it is." She beamed him a big smile and then got to her feet. "We'd better get busy."

He leaned back on his hands and looked up at her. "We're out of here at eleven, right?"

Was that going to be enough time? "Oh, I don't know. It's after nine now. Could we aim for one o'clock, do you think? I not only have to decide what to wear, I've got to have a little time to—"

"One is great."

"You'll call your mother and—"

"Jane. I've got my orders. Now get lost and give me a chance to carry them out."

* * *

Jane spoke with her father before she left for the bookstore. It took more than one call, but she finally reached him at the county courthouse. He wasn't exactly pleased, but at least he didn't shout at her or plead with her to change her mind—or tell her she had a fatal weakness for the wrong kind of man.

"You're an adult now, Jane. Your life is your own. I only hope you know what you're doing."

"I do know what I'm doing, Dad."

"Then I wish you and your new husband the best."

He was taking it so well, she considered inviting him along for the ceremony. But then she felt just uncomfortable enough at the idea that she didn't do it.

Really, the man was like a ghost in her life. A father *figure* and not much else. A good provider, always busy. It seemed to her that she thought of him...from a distance. Standing off to the side, not really involved in her life in any meaningful way.

He had stood by her bed, when she lost her child. She remembered him, looking down at her, a worried frown on his face. But she didn't remember him reaching out, to offer a hug or a loving kiss on the cheek, to smooth her hair or squeeze her hand the way most people's fathers would.

He'd been there for her graduation from Stanford, too. Had he hugged her then? Not that she could remember. He'd congratulated her, told her he was proud of her. She'd seen the approval in his eyes. She'd been pleased, she remembered. And satisfied.

Just as now she was satisfied to have his good

wishes for her marriage. She simply didn't feel close enough to him to want him there to walk her down the aisle.

Jane called Celia from the store. She and Aaron were still in town, at the New Venice Inn. They'd just returned to the inn to pack their own suitcases after seeing off the various Bravo relatives.

Celia shouted for pure joy when she heard the news—and quickly made plans with Aaron to reschedule their flight back to Las Vegas. They'd stay at the inn another night. And they'd follow Jane and Cade to Tahoe.

"Oh, Janey. I'm so happy for you. Have you called Jilly?"

"I was just about to."

"Does she know, about you and Cade?"

Jane sighed.

Celia said, "Do it now."

"Okay."

"Call me back."

"I will, I will." The line went dead and Jane dialed Jillian's number. She got a machine. She tried Jillian's cell phone. No answer there, either. So she left another message.

She called Celia again. "I couldn't reach Jillian. I left her two long messages, on her home phone and her cell, telling her all about what's going on."

"She'll be sulky when she hears you've been holding out about Cade."

"Oh, I know it."

"Not to mention heartbroken when she finds out she missed the wedding."

"Hey. You don't have to rub it in."

"Yes, I do. I'm still a little mad at you. You really should have told me."

"Sorry, Ceil. Truly, honestly, utterly sorry. Please accept my heartfelt apologies."

"I love it when you grovel. It happens so seldom— and don't worry. Jilly will be disappointed. But she'll live. And we'll take lots of pictures."

"Oh, that's right." Jane hadn't even thought of who was going to take pictures. Whatever chapel they chose would no doubt have portrait options. But she wanted lots of candid shots, too. "Bring that new camera of yours."

"I plan to."

"We're leaving for Tahoe at one. But you know, I was thinking, if you got to my house by noon—"

"Good idea. I'll help you get dressed. We can work with your hair—and by the way, what are you wearing?"

"I haven't decided yet. We'll figure out something."

"This is the part where we really need Jilly."

"We'll manage," said Jane. "Somehow." She felt a definite lump in her throat. "Ceil?"

"I'm here."

"Yeah. You are. And it means a lot. It's always meant a lot."

"Triple threat," said Celia, softly.

And Jane repeated, "Triple threat."

About ten minutes later, Caitlin burst in the front door of the shop. "Where's Jane? Jane, honey, where the hell are you?"

Laughing, Jane emerged from behind one of the center bookshelves. ''I'm right here, Caitlin. You don't have to shout.''

''I'll shout if I want to. I'll shout the place down. Get over here, come on.'' Caitlin held out her arms.

Jane found herself crushed against her future mother-in-law's lush, sequined bosom, that musky perfume Caitlin always wore making her head spin.

''Oh, I am so damn happy,'' Caitlin announced, hugging all the harder. ''I am one happy woman.'' Caitlin grabbed Jane by the shoulders and held her at arm's distance so she could look at her. ''My daughter-in-law. I don't believe it.''

Jane laughed. ''What? Should I pinch you?''

''Cade said I could go. Is that true? Can I go?''

''We'd love for you to go.''

''Oh, I am so happy.''

''I think you mentioned that already.''

''Have you noticed? My sons choose the absolute best women to marry.'' Caitlin cast a meaningful glance toward the register, where Madelyn was busy ringing up the first sale of the day. ''Come here a minute.'' She pulled Jane back among the shelves and whispered, ''I've got my fingers crossed that you're not gonna let any *troublemakers* mess things up for you.''

Jane squeezed Caitlin's arm. ''Don't worry. Please. I've already talked to the troublemakers.''

''And?''

''Consider them dealt with.''

Cade was upstairs in his bathroom squirting shaving cream into his hand when the doorbell rang.

He stuck his hand under the faucet to rinse off the froth of white stuff. Then he grabbed a towel.

The doorbell rang for the second time as he was zipping up his pants. He reached for the first shirt he saw—the one he'd worn yesterday—and made for the stairs, pulling it on and buttoning it up as he went.

The bell rang once more just as he was hauling open the front door.

Virginia Elliott stood on the other side.

"Please," she said. "I must speak with you."

Chapter Seventeen

The woman was neat and tidy as ever, not a hair out of place, her navy blue slacks and white shirt without a single wrinkle. But her gray eyes had a wild look in them, a burning look of furious determination.

Even without that scary look in her eyes, she would have made Cade damned nervous. She always had made him nervous. He couldn't remember her ever saying so much as a single word to him until five seconds ago. But whenever she looked his way—on the street when he was younger, through Jane's windows in the last several months—he'd seen the disapproval and disgust in her eyes, in the set of her narrow jaw, in the cold curl of her thin lips.

Today was the same as always—only more so.

"Mrs. Elliott," he said carefully, not wanting to

set her off if he could avoid it. "I'm sorry. Jane's not here."

"I didn't say I was looking for Jane. I want to talk to *you*." She cast that disapproving glance downward, toward his bare feet. Then she snapped her gaze up again. She didn't quite meet his eyes. She appeared to be studying the stubble he'd yet to shave off his jaw. "May I come in?"

No, he thought. *Bad idea. Go away.*

But he couldn't quite bring himself to shut the door in her face. She was Jane's mother. Someday, maybe, he'd find a way to get along with her. And he knew that Jane loved her, that Jane didn't really want to cut her off.

"I *said,* may I come in?"

He stepped back and gestured toward the entrance to the turret room.

"Thank you," she said, in a way that he knew didn't really mean Thank you at all. She entered his house and she hurried ahead of him to the room he'd indicated, the low heels of her well-made shoes tapping an angry rhythm across his floor.

She wouldn't sit down. She went to the circle of windows in the turret and stood with her back to them, as if she feared a surprise attack and wanted a view of the entire room, including the only way in or out. She had a little navy-blue purse with her and she held it in front of her, as if it was going to protect her from his evil self.

As if his evil self had any interest at all in getting near her. He stayed several feet away from her, near the leather sofa in the center of the room.

She didn't mince words. "I'm here to do whatever I have to do—beg you, *pay* you, whatever it takes—to convince you to leave my daughter alone."

Why the hell had he let her in here? "Mrs. Elliott—"

She jerked up a hand, fingers splayed, palm out. "No. I'm not finished. Please let me finish."

He felt kind of sick to his stomach. He didn't need this. He had enough damn nagging doubts of his own about what he and Jane were doing. He didn't need this smooth-haired, wild-eyed mother of hers making it worse.

"You know it can't work," Virginia Elliott said. "You know you're only going to break her poor heart. You're not a man who is cut out for marriage. You're only going to drag Jane down. She has a fatal weakness, for men like you. We both know that. What I'm sure you don't know, is what she's been through, all she's suffered."

There was a silence. One that echoed like a shout.

He realized she wanted him to speak now, to tell her how he didn't know what she was talking about. "As a matter of fact, Mrs. Elliott, I do know."

Her thin mouth pinched up tight. "You know." She scoffed the words.

He replied levelly. "That's what I said."

"She told you—the truth about that monster, Rusty Jenkins? About how he beat her? About how he killed her baby?"

"Mrs. Elliott—"

"I asked you a question—two questions, to be specific."

"Fine. Yes. She told me. About Rusty. And about how she lost her baby."

"Well," she said tightly. "Well, all right, then. All right then, you know."

"Yeah. I know."

"Then what *are* you, what kind of man are you, to go and ruin her life all over again?"

He opened his mouth—and then shut it without speaking. What the hell could he say to a loaded question like that?

And she was on a roll anyway. "I know, Cade Bravo, what you are. You are the child of an unholy union between a murderer and a—"

"Don't," he said very softly.

She must have seen in his eyes that he meant what said. Because she left that particular sentence unfinished. But *she* wasn't finished. Not by a long shot.

"All those women you've been with," she sneered. "The way you gamble to make your living, the brawls, the drunken crazy antics that have landed you in prison."

He couldn't let that pass. "Jail, Mrs. Elliott. I've been in jail. Never in prison."

"Oh. Well, all right. Jail and not prison. The point is, you've been arrested. The point is you're a drunk and a no-good and you'll end up betraying my daughter with some other woman. You'll end up breaking her heart and beating her up, just like—"

"I've heard enough."

"I am not finished."

"*I* am. I want you to go."

"I want you to—"

He took a step toward her. She let out a cry and held out her little blue purse, clutching it with both hands, an absurd makeshift shield against him. "Stop. Don't come near me."

"Just get the hell out. Get the hell out now."

She grabbed the purse close to her and she let out a cry. "I am begging you. Please. I can pay you. I can—"

He took another step.

She dashed to the side, circling the outer perimeter of the turret, keeping well away from him, quickly reaching the wide doorway that led to the front hall. He actually dared to hope she'd keep going. But she just couldn't do that, couldn't leave bad enough alone.

She turned in the doorway, her face twisting up into something that looked a lot like real agony. "Why?" she cried. "Why do you have to do this? Why do you—"

"Because I love her."

He said it and swallowed. Hard.

By God. It was true. He did. He loved Jane.

It had finally happened. To him. To Cade Bravo. He understood what love was now. Because he was in it. He was in it deep.

He said it again. "I love her. I love Jane."

"If you do," said Virginia, drawing her thin shoulders back and aiming that sharp chin high. "If you really do love her, then you'll realize you're no good for her. You'll want the very best for her. You'll let yourself see the parallels here, between yourself and Rusty Jenkins, between now and then. You'll see how much the same it is, the way it's all happening so suddenly, out of nowhere, you two running off to get married, right away, today.

"She has to do it that way, don't you see? She can't allow herself time to think about what she's doing. If she gave herself some time to think, we both know she'd change her mind."

"No," he said, hating the fact that what he was hearing made a sick kind of sense. "You don't know what you're talking about."

"Don't I? You think about it. And you'll see that I know what I'm saying. And when you see that, maybe you'll surprise us both. Maybe you'll do the right thing. Maybe you'll get out of her life and give her a chance to find a better man, the *right* man, the kind of man that she deserves."

Chapter Eighteen

Jane got back to her house at ten-thirty. She'd made all the calls that needed making. Madelyn had agreed to handle the shop by herself for the rest of the day and to stay for the book club meeting that evening.

Now the question was what to wear? And what about her hair? It was always a challenge. Maybe she could pile it up on top of her head somehow, or maybe try a few braids, little ones, at her temples, and pull the rest of it back and—

Jane let out a laugh. Her hair was something better handled with help. She could wait until Celia arrived to figure out what to do with it. Right now, she'd better make some clothing choices, then maybe she could indulge herself just a little with, say, a twenty-minute soak in a scented bath. And then she'd have to get to work on her makeup.

Cade's new black pickup was there, in front of his house.

She smiled to herself. And where else would it be? Right now, he would still be inside, getting ready. For their wedding.

Their wedding.

She could hardly believe it. She was marrying Cade Bravo. By tonight, she would be his wife.

Sometimes life could be so strange. So amazing.

So thoroughly wonderful.

She was seriously tempted to run over there, just for a minute, to steal a few quick kisses. But with the two of them, kisses always led to other things. And they had their whole lives ahead of them, together. There would be plenty of time for those other things that kisses led to. Right now, she had a lot to do and a limited time to do it in.

She got out of her van and ran up her front walk. The cosmos, which were getting a little bit past their prime now, seemed to turn their fading faces to her as she went by. The gazing balls twinkled, catching and reflecting the bright glare of the sun.

Inside, Cade's hat was still on the long front hall table, next to the vase he had given her. The flowers needed replacing. She'd have to cut some fresh ones.

Not today, of course. No time today.

But maybe tomorrow.

When she'd be Mrs. Cade Bravo.

She said it out loud, "Mrs. Cade Bravo. Jane Bravo." She liked it. It sounded good. She smiled some more, at herself this time.

She'd always thought that when she married again,

she'd keep her own name. Or maybe hyphenate. But now that she was actually headed for the altar, she didn't want to do that. It seemed important, to take Cade's name, because of who she was and who he was. Important that everyone understand she was proud to be his wife, to stand at his side.

Proud to be a Bravo.

Yes. It was the right choice, to take his name.

She shook herself—and laughed again. Here she was on her wedding day, with a million things to do, standing here staring at her beautiful mercury glass vase, thinking about cutting fresh flowers, pondering her choice to take Cade's name. Time to get cracking.

She headed for the stairs.

She had her foot on the bottom step when the front door opened behind her. She turned at the sound.

"Cade." She started for him, her happy smile blooming wider than before.

Two steps later, she was hesitating.

He hadn't shaved. He still wore that wrinkled shirt from yesterday. And his expression...

"Cade, what's happened?"

One corner of his mouth curled up. But it wasn't anything resembling a smile. It was more like a grimace, a look of pain.

She hurried toward him. "Oh, what's the matter? What's—"

He stuck his hands in the pockets of his rumpled pants and backed up a step. "Don't."

That single word said volumes. She stopped a few feet from him, midway between the stairs and the door. "What? Talk to me. Please."

o

"I've been giving this whole thing some serious thought."

Oh, this wasn't good. Not good at all. "All right." *Stay calm,* she thought, *stay reasonable.* "What have you been thinking? Tell me. I'm listening."

He glanced away, then dragged his gaze back to meet hers. "Look. It's not going to work, okay?"

"It?" she asked, as if she didn't already know, as if she couldn't see in those silver eyes exactly what he was trying to tell her.

He swore and let out a hard, impatient breath. "It. Us. Getting married. It was a crazy idea and it's not going to work. We're better off to call it quits here and now, before we go all the way through with it and make things that much worse."

She clasped her hands in front of her—in order to keep from reaching for him. "What happened? Something happened, didn't it?"

"Nothing happened." He said it too fast. She knew he was lying. "I had a little time to think, that's all, a little time to realize that we got carried away last night—that *I* got carried away, bringing up marriage. I never in a million years imagined you'd say yes."

In spite of the way her heart was aching, that almost made her smile. "But Cade. I *did* say yes."

He glared at her. "And you should have had sense enough not to."

"Cade…"

"Damn it. Will you stop that?"

"Stop what?"

"Just don't look at me like that, all right?"

"What is going on? What *happened?*"

"I told you. Nothing."

"But that doesn't make sense. When I left here this morning, you were all for the two of us getting married."

"I had my doubts, even then."

Now he told her. "If you had doubts, you could have shared them with me."

"Damn it, Jane. I'm sharing. I'm sharing right now. Just…accept what I'm saying, all right. We're not getting married. I'm calling it off."

"But—"

She cut herself off when she heard him mutter, "And you should be grateful."

She made herself count to three before she replied to that one. "Excuse me? I should be *grateful?*"

He made a low, impatient sound and rammed his fists deeper into his pockets. "Yeah. Grateful. I'm keeping you from making the second biggest mistake of your life."

She let out a wild laugh.

He scowled. "It's not funny."

"Sorry. I think it is. And thank you so much for *saving* me from myself."

"Go ahead. Razz me. You know I'm right."

"I don't know any such thing. And if marrying you would be my second worst mistake, I assume you mean the worst was marrying Rusty?"

"That's right. I'm bad. But I'm not *that* bad."

What was going on here? She still did not get it. "We've been through this. I though we settled it. You are nothing like Rusty."

"There are parallels. We both know it."

"What do you mean, parallels? You're not a criminal, you don't have a drug problem. You never hit a woman. I was eighteen and didn't know my own heart, when I married Rusty. Now I'm just about a decade older. I know what love is and I love you. I see the wonderful, steady, straight-ahead guy inside you, the guy you really are, the one you've worked so hard to be."

"You see what you want to see."

"No. I see what's really there. Maybe I thought there were parallels, for all those months I refused you, all those months I went against what my heart was trying to tell me. But now I know that was only on the surface. Deep down, where it counts, you're the right guy for me. And I truly do believe I'm the woman for you."

His expression had changed, softened. He was listening, *hearing* her. Hope struck sparks inside her, sparks that caught and flared.

He said, "I'm gone a lot. I have to go where the game is. You wouldn't like that."

"We could work that out. I can live with it. If you'd only be true to me, I'll get along, when you're not here. Lots of people have good marriages where one person travels. Salesmen. Truckers. They make it work."

"My income's not steady. I've been flat broke more than once."

"So? We'll get by. I'm hardly destitute. Together, we'll be fine." The urge to reach for him was powerful. She held it in check. "Oh, Cade. I'm not trying to tell you it's going to be a fairy tale. But it *will* be worth it. I know. I know it in my heart.''

He whispered her name. Hope flared even brighter, until it lit up the world.

But then he blinked. He shook his head. ''No.''

The shadow of loss encroached again. And she found she was pleading. ''Oh, no. Don't do this. Please, please don't do this….''

But his face was set now, his eyes hardened against her. ''It's the right thing.''

''It's not.''

''Jane. Face it. It *is* the same as with Rusty.''

''No, it's not.''

''Think about it, about the way it's happening. Us running off, eloping to Tahoe. Everything done in a big hurry. No time to think, no time to reconsider. It's way, way too fast.''

''Time,'' she said, grasping at straws now—and knowing it. ''Time. Is that it? You're scared and you need a little time to—''

''Jane. Give it up.''

''No. I won't. I can't. I don't understand.''

''Sure, you do. You just don't like it.''

''It doesn't add up. I know you called Caitlin. You told her we were getting married, told her she could come with us to Tahoe. Why would you do that, if you were having serious doubts?''

''I didn't come to my senses until after I'd called her, that's all.''

''No. I don't buy that. I don't—''

''Jane. Enough. Someday you'll look back and feel nothing but relief that I did this.''

"That's not true."

"You'll admit to yourself that you've got a fatal weakness for guys like me and you'll—"

"Wait." She had it. She understood.

"What?"

"A *fatal weakness*. That's what you said."

"Yeah. So?"

"You've been talking to my mother."

"Jane—"

"You have. I know you have. She said those exact words to me, too. She said I had a *fatal weakness* for the wrong kind of man."

He glanced away again. Away, and then back. "Jane…"

"Uh-uh. Those are her words I heard coming out of your mouth. She got to you. She got to you good. And you let her." That really hurt. "Oh, Cade. How could you listen to her? How could you *believe* her? She's a fanatic, the way she hates Caitlin—and anyone connected to Caitlin. She's the next thing to a mental case over it. You have to see that. You can't let her—"

"Jane. It doesn't matter, who I talked to, what was said."

"Oh, yes it does. It matters a lot."

"No. I mean what I'm telling you. It's over. Goodbye." He started to turn.

Desperate, she cried out, "But what about last night? What if I'm pregnant?"

That stopped him. He faced her once more and looked her up and down. And then he grunted. "Nice try."

"Don't you *grunt* at me. I thought it was important to you, that your babies have your name."

"It was only one night, Jane. We both know it's damn doubtful you're pregnant from one night."

"But it *is* possible."

"Fine. If it turns out you're pregnant, all right. I'll marry you."

She could have strangled him. "Oh, hey, mister. Don't put yourself out."

"Bye, Jane." He turned again for the door, reaching to grab his hat off the long table as he went by.

She couldn't bear it. She rushed for him, caught his outstretched arm. "Oh, wait!"

"Damn it, Jane." He jerked free.

The action caught her off-balance. She staggered into the table. Before she could steady herself, the table lifted on two legs and Cade's hat, the carnival glass bowl and her beautiful mercury glass gazing-ball vase were sliding to the floor.

The hat and the bowl landed without incident.

The vase hit with a crash and shattered. Glass flew. Mercury slithered everywhere.

"Oh, no," Jane whispered. "Oh, no, no, no…" She had found her feet. It only felt as if the world had dropped out from under her.

Cade bent, grabbed his hat and slapped it against his thigh. A few bits of broken glass tinkled to the floor. "Keep me around." He settled the hat on his head. "See what else gets broken."

She was done, she realized. Finished. Out of reasons why he should stay. She stared into those hard silver eyes. She was thinking that, under no circumstances, was he going to see her cry.

Finally she nodded. ''All right. You want to go, then go.''

He didn't wait around for her to change her mind.

Chapter Nineteen

Once he was gone, Jane stood in the foyer staring at her shut door and let herself cry, let the tears stream down her face, let the hard sobs take her.

After a while, she got tired of just standing there bawling. So she picked up the carnival glass bowl and carried it to the kitchen. She left it on the counter and then she went out to the service porch and got a pair of rubber gloves and a broom and a dust mop.

Sobbing as she worked, she picked up the half-dead flowers first, then the scattered shards of glass. She swept up the smaller pieces and blotted up the water. Finally, she put on her rubber gloves and chased the mercury around the floor, rolling the beads with her dustpan to join with the other beads, gathering the slippery, silvery stuff until she had one slinky, quivery mass of it. She coaxed the mass onto her dustpan with the edge of a ruler and then she managed to transfer it to a Mason jar.

Still crying, sniffing and sobbing, tears running down her face, she screwed the lid on the jar. Then she held it up and stared at the quivering quicksilver inside, thinking how what she saw was just like Cade, that he was a silver-eyed charmer. Hazardous material. So hard to hold.

By then, it was eleven-thirty. She took off her gloves and washed her hands and her face. She blew her nose and combed her hair. When Celia and Aaron arrived at five minutes of noon, she was sitting at her kitchen table, staring out the bay window.

She heard the knocking at the front door, but she didn't answer. She knew eventually her friend would just come on in.

"Omigod, what's happened?" Celia cried when she and Aaron entered the kitchen. Jane turned and looked at her.

Celia said, "Aaron, darling. I think Jane and I need to be alone now."

He turned to go.

Before he could take more than a step, Jane said, "Aaron. I need a favor."

"Anything."

"Cade invited your mother to come with us to Tahoe. It's not going to happen. I wonder if you could—"

"No problem. I'll cut her off at the pass."

She thanked him and he left. Then Celia held out loving arms. With a heavy sob, Jane went into them.

Celia made tender noises and held on tight as Jane indulged herself in another good cry.

But she couldn't cry forever. After a while, she blew her nose again and splashed cold water on her face. Celia made them some green tea and they sat at the table, sipping, while Jane told all.

"Something has got to be done about that mother of yours," Celia said when the sad story was through.

"Tell me about it."

"What are your plans?"

"I'm going to have a talk with her. It may be my *last* talk with her. But I'm going to get a few things straight with her. I just need to ask my father a few questions first."

Celia blinked those big hazel eyes. "Your father? You *never* talk with your father."

"I know. But I'm talking with him now. I want to hear his side of what happened way back when. I heard the story from Aunt Sophie. And I'm reasonably sure she got it right. My mother is never going to talk about it—except obliquely, always blaming Caitlin. Caitlin will only say that she never slept with my father. I believe her. But I want to hear it from him, too. I want to hear what he says happened. I want to understand how my mother could hate another woman so much that she'd be willing to ruin her own daughter's happiness for the sake of that hatred."

Celia winced. "I've gotta ask."

"Go ahead."

"Well, so how's this going to help you get Cade back?"

"It probably won't. I guess maybe I'm hoping for the impossible. That I'll learn something from my father that will help my mother see the light. That I'll get her to admit to Cade how wrong she was."

"Jane. I have to tell you. I can't see that happening, ever."

"Yeah, okay, neither can I. But I have to try."

Her father kept an office on State Street. He agreed to meet with her there that evening at six.

She sat in the green leather guest chair opposite his mahogany desk and she told him that Cade had broken it off with her after Virginia had been to see him.

Her father sat back in his huge button-tucked swivel chair. "I'm sorry that it didn't work out as you'd hoped."

Did she buy that? Hardly. "Are you, Dad?"

"Well. As I told you on the phone this morning, you're an adult and you are fully qualified to make your own decisions. The time is long past when I felt I could tell you what choices to make."

"Maybe you should tell that to my mother."

"Jane. You know very well I can't tell your mother anything."

Jane felt all the old resentments bubbling to the surface. She wanted to ask what it *was* with them? Why did they stay together? How could they live the way that they did?

But that wasn't why she'd come.

"I have a few questions for you, Dad. I'd really appreciate honest answers. It would help me to understand what's really going on here."

His severe expression got bleaker than ever. "What is it, Jane?"

"I want to know about you and Caitlin Bravo. I want to know what happened between you. And I want to know why my mother never forgave Caitlin for it."

Her father said nothing for several endless seconds. Jane thought he was going to tell her that he wanted her to leave.

But then he said, "Your aunt Sophie told me she'd explained it all to you."

Jane sat up straighter. "Wait a minute. Aunt Sophie *told* you that she told me?"

He actually chuckled. It was a pretty rusty sound, but then he didn't laugh often. "I confess. I knew you were close to Sophie. And I never did seem to know where to start when it came to trying to communicate with you. So now and then, I would ask my sister—how you were doing, what was going on in your life. You know your aunt. She never pulled any punches." His dark eyes were so sad. "I miss Sophie. A lot."

Jane had thought she was cried out, that she couldn't shed another tear if she'd wanted to. Still, she felt the tightening of emotion in her throat, the pressure behind her eyes. "I miss her, too—and yes. Aunt Sophie did talk to me about it. She said that you fell for Caitlin, but that Caitlin refused you, told you to go back to your wife. So you left Mom and tried again to get Caitlin to give you a chance, but Caitlin still sent you away."

Her father shrugged. "That's about the size of it.

It was a tough time. I did love your mother, but she was…difficult. So high-strung. A perfectionist. And distant, a lot of the time. And then she had you. You were everything to her. Once you were born, she had nothing left to give to me. I started going to the High-grade. Caitlin was kind to me. She would listen while I yammered on about how miserable I was, how my wife didn't have any time for me…'' He closed his eyes and let out a long breath. When he opened them again, Jane could see he didn't intend to say much more. "It was a long time ago. In the end, I went back to your mother. We patched it up, more or less. Now, we get along well enough. We're used to what we have together. And to what we don't have.''

"But of the three of you, Caitlin is clearly the in-nocent one. You're telling me she never encouraged you, right?''

"That's right. She was kind to me. And she lis-tened to me. At the time, I wanted to believe that she saw me as a man, that she was attracted. But looking back, no. She was a good bartender with a big heart. She felt sorry for me.''

"Then why does Mom blame her?''

"Surely that's obvious.''

"Not to me.''

"Your mother has way too much pride. If she blames herself for driving me away, then she's got to swallow her pride and deal with her own shortcom-ings. She's not ready for that. On the other hand, with all that pride of hers, if she blames *me,* she'd have to divorce me.''

"And being the wife of Judge Clifford Elliott is very, very important to her."

Her father didn't respond to that. There was no need to. They both knew it was true.

Jane said, "You're saying that Caitlin's her scapegoat."

"That's right." He sat forward. "And what good does hearing all this do you, really?"

"I don't know, Dad. I just wanted to understand."

"I'd like to give you some advice. I don't expect you to take it, but for once I'd like to be able to say I told you the things I really thought you should know."

"Please. I want to hear it."

"Leave your mother alone now. Just…stay clear of her. Don't do the most tempting thing. Don't feel you have to confront her or tell her off for what she did to you. And please don't imagine you're going to change her, to get her on your side when it comes to the man you love. It won't happen."

"But I thought—"

He shook his head. "No. You're not going to change her. Only she can do that. Eventually she'll come to you. Because in spite of how misguided she is, she loves you. Very much. When she does come to you, you'll have some tough choices to make. But right now, leave her alone. Right now, you have something else you should be dealing with."

Jane answered softly. "You know, Dad. You're right."

"I must admit, the more I think about it, the more

I become accustomed to the idea of you and Cade Bravo together.''

Jane gulped down those pesky, persistent tears. ''Oh, Dad. You do?''

He nodded. ''He's cleaned up his act in the past few years.''

''He has. He truly has.''

''Seems to me someone like him might be just right for you. Where is he now?''

Jane shrugged. She supposed he'd left town again. His truck had vanished from the curb in front of his house. ''I *will* find him. Somehow.''

''That's what I like to hear.''

''And, Dad, when I do, when I work all this out, will you walk me down the aisle?''

''I thought you'd never ask.''

Jane's phone was ringing when she got back to her house. She didn't want to talk to anyone, so she let the machine get it. The machine was in the kitchen. But she'd left the volume up, so she heard Caitlin's voice all the way from the front hall.

''Jane? Damn it, Jane. Pick up...''

Jane sighed and moved toward the voice on the machine—not to answer it but to get a glass of iced tea from the fridge.

''Jane. You listen to me, Jane. What the hell is going on? Nobody's telling me a damn thing. As usual, I'm the mushroom in the crowd, kept in the dark. Fed a lot of crap. Aaron comes over here at noon and tells me the wedding's off. *What?* I said. *Why?* Aaron doesn't answer. He just orders me to stay put, to leave you alone, to mind my own business. Says you want it that way. That the baby doll is with you and you're going to be fine...."

Jane opened the fridge, took out the tea.

"Fine? *Fine?* How can you be fine, if you love my son and you were on your way to Tahoe and now you're *not* on your way to Tahoe, you've called it off. Or *he's* called it off. Not that I would know. And don't think I didn't ask him."

Jane got down a tall class, stuck it under the ice chute in the refrigerator door. For a few seconds, the clatter of the cubes drowned out whatever Caitlin was saying.

But then Jane could hear her again.

"...wouldn't tell me squat. Just said, 'Mind your own business, Ma. It didn't work out for Jane and me.' Then he heads for the back room and gets himself a game going. He—"

Jane grabbed for the phone. "Caitlin. Caitlin?"

"'Bout time you picked up."

"He's there, is that what you're saying? Cade is there? At the Highgrade?"

"Well, hell yes, he's here."

"Don't let him go anywhere."

"Honey, he's in the middle of a card game. A herd of mean mustangs couldn't drag him away."

Five minutes later, Jane entered the Highgrade through the back door. She raced down the long back hall. When she emerged into the central game room, she spotted Caitlin just coming out of the café, grabbing menus to seat the next group of customers who waited on the long bench opposite the high desk with the cash register on it.

Caitlin spotted her and pointed toward the entrance to the bar. "Through there, to the back room." Caitlin smiled at her customers, "Come on, folks. This way."

Jane went the other way, into the dimly lit bar.

Bertha Slider was serving the drinks, her gray-streaked red braids wrapped in a corona around her head. A few regulars sat on the stools, hunched over their drinks. They glanced her way, shrugged and went back to nursing whatever it was they were drinking.

"Hey, Jane." Pinky Cleeves, who'd been in Jane's class in school, raised her pool cue in a salute. Jane gave her nod.

Jane spoke to Bertha. "The back room?"

Bertha tipped her crown of braids toward a door deep in the shadows beyond the second pool table. "But I wouldn't interrupt, if I were you," she said under her breath.

"Thanks for the warning." Jane turned for the door. She felt the sudden silence as she strode the length of the room. The regulars were watching. Neither Pinky nor her opponent had turned back to their game.

Jane reached the door, raised her hand to knock— and changed her mind. She grabbed the door handle and gave it a turn.

In the smoky recess beyond, five men sat at a round felt-topped table. One of them was Cade.

"Hey," one of the other men said. "Close the damn door, will ya? We're busy in here."

"Yeah," said another. And another added, "Do it now."

The first man shouted, "Close the door! What are you, deaf?"

Cade didn't say anything. There were several tall stacks of poker chips in front of him. He still wore the rumpled clothes from yesterday. That straw cowboy hat shadowed his eyes.

Jane said, "I want to talk to you, Cade. I'm not leaving until I do." He just sat there, unmoving. She could feel his eyes on her beneath the brim of the hat. Jane cleared her throat. "I wonder if you gentlemen would mind getting out?"

There was a silence. A couple of the men mumbled profanities and grumbled some more about how she ought to get out and shut the door.

But then one of them laughed. "Hey. I'm about bust anyway." He threw his cards down. "You can make it up to me later, Bravo."

Cade made a grunting noise. It could have meant anything.

The man scooped his few chips into his hand and turned for the door. "Er, 'scuse me, ma'am." Jane stepped out of the way and he moved past her into the main part of the bar.

The other men—except Cade, who maintained a nerve-racking silence—muttered a few more rude epithets. Then a second one stood up. And the third. And the fourth. Each took a moment to collect the chips in front of him. Then, one by one, they filed out, headed for the cage at the end of the bar. Bertha was back there now, with the light on, ready to settle up.

As soon as the fourth man left the small room, Jane stepped in and pulled the door shut behind her. Cade just sat there, across the table, regarding her coolly from beneath the brim of his hat. Jane had her back against the door. Her heart was beating too fast and the smoke in the room stung her eyes.

Oh, what was he thinking? Why didn't he say something?

And right then, he did. "I was winning that game, Jane."

She drew herself up. "Too bad. That game is over."

"Oh, is it?"

I love you. Please say you love me back…

No such luck.

"Go on, Jane. Go home. We've got nothing more to say to each other. I'm no good for you and it's time we accepted that, time we started getting over each other."

"No. No, it isn't. What it's time for is time you stopped acting like an idiot, Cade Bravo. It's time you told me you love me. Time you admitted that your heart is mine."

"You're living in a fool's dream."

"No. No, I'm not. I've been thinking. And I think I've finally figured it out. What happened, with my mother. How she got to you, what she said."

"Jane—"

"Oh, come on. You can take it. You can listen to my theory."

"There's no point in—"

"She rubbed it in, didn't she? How much you're like Rusty? How I've got this big *problem* with falling for messed up men. How it's the same, our eloping, and my running off with Rusty. She got you doubting. She got to that hurt kid inside you, the one who had to listen to folks calling him a little bastard. And then she got you to admit that you love me. And *then* she told you that if you really *did* love me, you'd leave me alone."

He didn't move. And he didn't speak.

She said, "I do know. That you love me. I wish you had told me, instead of my mother. But it doesn't matter, if you say the words. Or if you don't. I know you love me. As I love you. And walking away from me isn't going to change that. Leaving me isn't going to make it all better. It's only going to break both our hearts."

He moved then. But only to throw down his hand.

She stepped forward.

"No." He shoved back his chair and stood.

She knew he was going to go, walk around the table, right past her—and out of the room. She put out both hands. "Listen. Let's talk this over. Please. Let's not be so hasty. Let's settle down, here."

He muttered her name. He was shaking his head.

Desperately she cast about for a way to keep him there. "How about this? How about I play you? Three hands. Uh, blackjack, okay? I mean, I know how to play that. Sort of. I do."

He said her name again—and she could have sworn he almost smiled.

"Look. Just sit down. Just shuffle and deal. Here's the thing. Here's my offer. Two out of three hands. If I win, you marry me."

"And if I win?"

"I'll leave." For now, she amended silently. I'll leave *for now*.

He pushed his hat back a little and gave her one of those long, slow sizing-up kind of looks. Then he dropped to his chair again. He began gathering up the cards.

She sat across from him, her heart pounding like mad, watching him shuffle—oh that was a thing of beauty, the way that man could handle those cards.

"Cut."

She did.

He put the bottom half on top and took the first card—a two of diamonds—and placed it face-up at the bottom of the deck. Then he dealt four cards in quick succession, one face down to each of them, a second facedown to her and one face-up to himself. His card showing was an ace of spades.

She peeked at her own. A six of clubs and a ten of hearts. She knew a little bit about odds. And she'd read somewhere that you shouldn't ask for another card if you had sixteen already. But he had an *ace*.

She said, "Hit me."

When he dealt her a queen of hearts, she uttered a very bad swear word.

He smiled at her then—and turned over his first card. King of clubs. Twenty-one.

"How did you do that?" she demanded. "Did you cheat?"

He gave her a patient look. "*You* want to deal?"

"Uh. No. You go right ahead."

He did. And it happened all over again. That time he had the ace of hearts showing. She got a seven of diamonds and a nine of clubs. She stayed, that time.

And he flipped over his bottom card. Jack of spades.

And that was it.

He gave her a crooked smile. "It's over, Jane."

"You did cheat, didn't you?"

He shrugged. "Better pay up."

What else could she do? She stood. "I would like to say one more thing, before I go. I want to say, again, that I love you. And I'm sorry for the rotten things my mother said to you. But I am not my mother and I know the kind of man you really are. A good one. And a steady one. And the only one for me. And as soon as you're willing to admit that I'm the only one for you, I do sincerely hope you will come over to my house and knock on my door." She turned.

And he said, "Hold on a minute…"

And something snapped inside her.

She whirled on him, fed up with fighting for him when all he did was turn her down. "*What?*" she shouted. "What the hell do you want?"

And he grinned at her. "Care to try for three out of five?"

She stared. And then she gulped and then she

asked, very carefully, ''Are you saying what I think you're saying?''

''I'm saying you're right. I'm saying I love you. I'm saying let's do it. Let's get married.''

''Oh, God. You mean it.''

''You're damned right I do.''

She let out a cry of pure joy and she ran around that table and threw herself into his waiting arms. He gathered her close and his mouth came down on hers and when they finally came up for air, she said, ''Tahoe. Tomorrow. No backing out.''

And he said, ''However you want it, Jane. That's how it will be.''

Epilogue

Jillian called that night. When she heard the news she got in her car and she drove straight to New Venice. The next morning, she did wonderful things with Jane's hair.

They all caravanned to Tahoe, Cade and Jane in the lead, with Aaron and Celia and Jillian in the next car, Caitlin and Will in the Trans Am, and Jane's father in his Cadillac taking up the rear.

The rumor mill went wild. Everyone said that Jane Elliott had made the same big mistake all over again, taken another thoroughly unsuitable mate. They said it would never last.

But Jane didn't care what they said. She knew that in Cade Bravo she'd found much more than she'd ever dared dream of. She'd found a man she could count on, her very best friend—and a lover who set her body on fire. She knew that their union would last them both a lifetime.

As for Virginia, Jane refused to speak to her for two full years. But then the first baby came—a daughter they named Sophie Elizabeth. Cade couldn't stand it. He went and got Virginia and brought her to the hospital.

Jane was adamant. "I don't want to see you or talk to you," she said, "until you apologize to my mother-in-law." And she turned her face to the wall.

Virginia Elliott held out for three more days. And then she went to the Highgrade and asked to speak with Caitlin. No one ever knew what words passed between those two women in Caitlin's small dark office in the back of the saloon.

But after that, Virginia and Caitlin were always civil to each other. Jane allowed Cade to bring Virginia to the house on Green Street—Aunt Sophie's house, which was the one they had decided to live in—and Virginia Elliott held her first grandchild at last.

After that, folks said, there was a change in Virginia. A softening, a new gentleness. A mildness of spirit folks found very appealing. Clifford began spending more time at home.

Cade Bravo remained a professional gambler. He won and lost three fortunes in the next forty years. He loved his work and he loved his wife—and he loved the five children she eventually gave him.

And when Cade taught their grandchildren how to play blackjack, he also told them the tale of how their grandma gambled for his heart—and lost.

"Well, Grandpa," said silver-eyed ten-year-old Cait. "If she lost, how come you got married anyway?"

"Sweetheart," Cade replied. "Your grandpa is a lot of things. But stupid isn't one of them."

* * * * *

Don't forget to look out for the next Bravo bachelor's story—Scrooge and the Single Girl—in December 2003.

SILHOUETTE®
SPECIAL EDITION™

AVAILABLE FROM 17TH OCTOBER 2003

GOOD HUSBAND MATERIAL Susan Mallery
Hometown Heartbreakers

When Kari Asbury revisited her home town she never expected to bump into ex-fiancé Sheriff Gage Reynolds. But could Kari find the courage to overcome their past and stand by the man she'd always loved?

TALL, DARK AND IRRESISTIBLE Joan Elliott Pickart
The Baby Bet: MacAllister's Gifts

Ryan Sharpe was blatantly masculine, sexy and…irresistible. He could be with anyone, but his passionate pursuit told Carolyn he wanted *only* her. Dare Carolyn believe he'd still want her when he learned her secret?

MY SECRET WIFE Cathy Gillen Thacker
The Deveraux Legacy

A secret sex-only marriage was the only way Dr Gabe Deveraux knew to help best friend Maggie Calloway have a baby. But soon Gabe was forced to admit the truth—he'd secretly loved Maggie for years.

AN AMERICAN PRINCESS Tracy Sinclair

When Shannon Blanchard won TV's hottest game show, she never dreamed that her prize of two weeks at a royal castle would change her life. Until she set eyes on tall, dark and dangerously attractive Prince Michel de Mornay…

LT KENT: LONE WOLF Judith Lyons

Journalist Angie Rose wanted to unveil the hero…the mysterious millionaire that was Lt Jason Kent. But how could she expose Jason's secrets when their passion—*her heart*—revealed they were meant to be together?

THE STRANGER SHE MARRIED Crystal Green
Kane's Crossing

Two years ago Rachel Shane's husband vanished. Then, without warning, a rugged stranger with familiar eyes sauntered into her life professing amnesia. He was *all*-male and every inch a dangerous temptation…

1003/23a

NORA ROBERTS

Nora Roberts shows readers the lighter side of love in the Big Apple in this fun and romantic volume.

Truly Madly
MANHATTAN

Two fabulous stories about the city that never sleeps...
Local Hero & Dual Image

Available from 17th October 2003

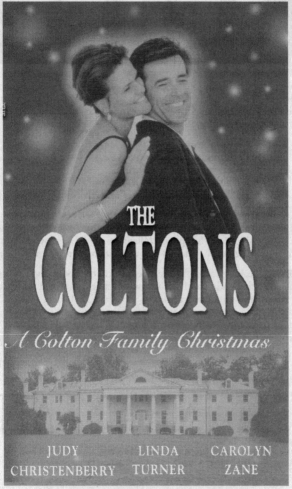

4 FREE

books and a surprise gift!

We would like to take this opportunity to thank you for reading this Silhouette® book by offering you the chance to take FOUR more specially selected titles from the Special Edition™ series absolutely FREE! We're also making this offer to introduce you to the benefits of the Reader Service™—

- ★ FREE home delivery
- ★ FREE gifts and competitions
- ★ FREE monthly Newsletter
- ★ Exclusive Reader Service discount
- ★ Books available before they're in the shops

Accepting these FREE books and gift places you under no obligation to buy, you may cancel at any time, even after receiving your free shipment. Simply complete your details below and return the entire page to the address below. *You don't even need a stamp!*

YES! Please send me 4 free Special Edition books and a surprise gift. I understand that unless you hear from me, I will receive 6 superb new titles every month for just £2.90 each, postage and packing free. I am under no obligation to purchase any books and may cancel my subscription at any time. The free books and gift will be mine to keep in any case.

E3ZEE

Ms/Mrs/Miss/Mr ....Initials....................................
BLOCK CAPITALS PLEASE

Surname ....

Address ....

....

....Postcode................................

Send this whole page to:
UK: FREEPOST CN81, Croydon, CR9 3WZ
EIRE: PO Box 4546, Kilcock, County Kildare (stamp required)